KU-634-751

Quickly, bravely, she said, 'For the record, Joe, it isn't true.'

He turned, looking at her intently. 'What do you mean?'

His blue eyes seemed to penetrate all the way to her soul. Her heart began to gallop. She couldn't back down now that she'd begun.

'What you said before—that I can't bear the sight of you—it's not true.' *So not true.*

'That's the way it comes across.'

'I know. I'm sorry. Really sorry.'

She could feel the sudden stillness in him, almost as if she'd shot him. He was staring at her, his eyes burning. With doubt?

Ellie's eyes were stinging. She didn't want to cry, but she could no longer see the paddocks. Her heart was racing.

She almost told Joe that she actually *fancied* the sight of him. Very much. Too much. *That* was her problem. That was why she was tense.

But it was too late for personal confessions. Way too late. Years and years too late.

Instead she said, 'I know I've been stupidly tense…about…*everything*, but it's certainly not because I can't stand the sight of you.' *Quite the opposite…*

Dear Reader

This is not a story about conflict and war. It's a story that touches on the hardship, loneliness and stress that many families bravely face when soldiers are sent overseas on active service.

I've loved writing Joe and Ellie's (and Jacko's) story. I felt very involved as I explored their emotional conflicts and worked to find a realistic way for them to achieve their happy ending. Thank heavens for romance, where everything works out OK.

I've lived for most of my adult life in Townsville, the largest Australian city in the tropics and home to a large army base. It's impossible to live in Townsville without being aware of the fantastic role that servicemen and women play in the local community and in the world at large.

They have served on UN peace-keeping missions across the globe, provided rapid response to our neighbours in times of natural disaster, helped to rebuild war-ravaged communities and, sadly, made the supreme sacrifice in war zones.

At the time of writing troops were coming home and television news was showing emotional and heart-warming scenes as soldiers were reunited with their loved ones.

But in real life not all stories have a happy ending, and the joyous scenes at our city airport were tempered by the fact that twenty widows and forty-five children were not able to welcome back their husbands and fathers.

For all these reasons I am honoured that I'm now able to share Joe and Ellie's story with you.

Warmest wishes

Barbara Hannay

SECOND CHANCE WITH HER SOLDIER

BY

BARBARA HANNAY

MILLS & BOON

All the characters in this book have no existence outside the imagination of the author, and have no relation whatsoever to anyone bearing the same name or names. They are not even distantly inspired by any individual known or unknown to the author, and all the incidents are pure invention.

All Rights Reserved including the right of reproduction in whole or in part in any form. This edition is published by arrangement with Harlequin Enterprises II BV/S.à.r.l. The text of this publication or any part thereof may not be reproduced or transmitted in any form or by any means, electronic or mechanical, including photocopying, recording, storage in an information retrieval system, or otherwise, without the written permission of the publisher.

® and TM are trademarks owned and used by the trademark owner and/or its licensee. Trademarks marked with ® are registered with the United Kingdom Patent Office and/or the Office for Harmonisation in the Internal Market and in other countries.

Reading and writing have always been a big part of **Barbara Hannay**'s life. She wrote her first short story at the age of eight for the Brownies' writer's badge. It was about a girl who was devastated when her family had to move from the city to the Australian Outback.

Since then, a love of both city and country lifestyles has been a continuing theme in Barbara's books and in her life. Although she has mostly lived in cities, now that her family has grown up and she's a full-time writer she's enjoying a country lifestyle.

Barbara and her husband live on a misty hillside in Far North Queensland's Atherton Tableland. When she's not lost in the world of her stories she's enjoying farmers' markets, gardening clubs and writing groups, or preparing for visits from family and friends.

Barbara records her country life in her blog, *Barbwired*, and her website is: www.barbarahannay.com

Recent books by Barbara Hannay:

MIRACLE IN BELLAROO CREEK*
THE CATTLEMAN'S SPECIAL DELIVERY
FALLING FOR MR MYSTERIOUS
RUNAWAY BRIDE
BRIDESMAID SAYS, 'I DO!'
RANCHER'S TWINS: MUM NEEEDED
MOLLY COOPER'S DREAM DATE
A MIRACLE FOR HIS SECRET SON
EXECUTIVE: EXPECTING TINY TWINS
THE CATTLEMAN'S ADOPTED FAMILY
THE BRIDESMAID'S BABY

*Bellaroo Creek!

**Other titles by this author are available in eBook format.
Visit www.millsandboon.co.uk**

PROLOGUE

CORPORAL JOE MADDEN waited two whole days before he opened the email from his wife.

Avoidance was not Joe's usual MO. It went against everything he'd learned in his military training. *Strike swiftly* was the Australian Commandos' motto, and yet…here he was in Afghanistan, treating a rare message from Ellie as if it were more dangerous than an improvised explosive device.

Looming divorce could do that to a guy.

The fact that Joe had actually offered to divorce Ellie was irrelevant. After too many stormy years of marriage, he'd known that his suggestion was both necessary and fair, but the break-up certainly hadn't been easy or painless.

Now, in his tiny hut in Tarin Kot, Joe scanned the two other email messages that had arrived from Australia overnight. The first was his aunt's unhelpful reminder that she never stopped worrying about him. The other was a note from one of his brothers. This, at least, was glib and slightly crude and elicited a wry chuckle from Joe.

But he was left staring at Ellie's as yet unopened email with its gut-churning subject heading: *Crunch Time*.

Joe knew exactly what this meant. The final divorce

papers had arrived from their solicitor and Ellie was impatient to serve him with them.

Clearly, she was no longer prepared to wait till the end of his four years in the army, even though his reasons for suggesting the delay had been entirely practical.

Joe knew no soldier was safe in Afghanistan, and if he was killed while he and Ellie were still married, she would receive an Army widow's full entitlements. Financially, at least, she would be OK.

Surely this was important? The worst could so easily happen here. In his frequent deployments, Joe faced daily, if not hourly, danger and he'd already lost two close mates, both of them brilliant, superbly trained soldiers. Death was a real and ever-present danger.

Joe had felt compelled to offer Ellie a safety net, so he'd been reassured to know that, whatever happened to him, she would be financially secure. But, clearly, getting out of their marriage now was more important to her than the long-term benefits.

Hell, she probably had another bloke lined up in the wings. Please, let it be anyone but that damn potato farmer her mother had hand-picked for her.

But, whatever Ellie's reasons, the evidence of her impatience sat before Joe on the screen.

Crunch Time.

There was no point in avoiding this any longer. The coffee Joe had recently downed turned sour as he grimly clicked on the message.

It was a stinking-hot day at Karinya Station in Far North Queensland. The paddocks were parched and the cattle hungry as Ellie Madden delivered molasses to the empty troughs. The anxious beasts pushed and shoved at her, trying to knock the molasses barrel out of her hands, so of course she was as sticky and grimy as a candy bar dropped in dirt by the time she arrived back at the homestead.

Her top priority was to hit the laundry and scrub up to her elbows. That done, she strode through the kitchen, grabbed a jug of chilled water from the fridge, filled a glass and gulped it down. Taking another glassful with her to the study, she remained standing in her molasses-smeared jeans as she fired up her laptop.

Tension vibrated and buzzed inside her as the latest messages downloaded. Surely Joe would send his answer today?

She was so sick with apprehension she closed her eyes and held her breath until she heard the ping of the final message's arrival. When she forced herself to peek at the screen again, she felt an immediate plunge of disappointment.

Nothing from Joe.

Not a word.

For fraught minutes, she stood staring at the screen, as if somehow she could *will* another email to appear. She hit 'send and receive', just to be sure.

Still nothing.

Why hadn't he replied? What was the hold-up? Even if he'd been out on a patrol, he was usually back at camp within a day or two.

A ripple of fear trembled through her like chilling wind over water.

Surely he couldn't have been injured? Not Joe.

The Army would have contacted her.

Don't think about that.

Ever since her husband had joined the Army, Ellie had schooled herself to stomp on negative thoughts. She knew other Army couples had secret 'codes' for when they talked about anything dangerous, but she and Joe had lost that kind of closeness long ago. Now she quickly searched for a more likely explanation.

Joe was probably giving her email careful thought. After all, it would have come as a shock, and no doubt he was weighing up the pros and cons of her surprising proposal.

Wanting to reassure herself, Ellie reread the email she'd sent him, just to make sure that it still sounded reasonable.

She'd tried to put her case concisely and directly, keeping it free of emotion, which was only fitting now they'd agreed to divorce. Even so, as she read, she found herself foolishly trying to imagine how Joe would feel as her message unfolded.

Hi Joe,
I hope all is well with you.

I'm writing on a practical matter. I've had another invoice from the fertility clinic, you see, and so I've been thinking again about the frozen embryos. (Surprise, surprise.)

Joe, I know we signed that form when we started the programme, agreeing that, in the case of divorce, we would donate any of our remaining embryos to another infertile couple. But I'm sorry—I'm having misgivings about that.

I've given it a lot of thought, Joe. Believe me, a LOT of thought.

I'd like to believe I would be generous enough to

hand over our embryos to a more deserving couple, but I can't help thinking of those little frozen guys as MY babies.

I've thought around and around this, Joe, and I've decided that I really do want to have that one last try at IVF. I know you will probably be horrified. You'll tell me that I'm setting myself up for another round of disappointment. I know this will come as a shock to you, and possibly a disappointment as well.

However, if by some amazing miracle I did become pregnant, I wouldn't expect to change our plans re the divorce. I promise I wouldn't try to use the baby to hold on to you, or anything manipulative like that.

As you know from past experience, success is EXTREMELY UNLIKELY, but I can't go ahead with IVF without your consent and I wouldn't want to, so obviously I'm very keen to hear your thoughts.

In the meantime, stay safe, Joe.

All the very best,

Ellie

Joe felt as if a grenade had exploded inches from his face.

I know this will come as a shock to you...

Hell, yeah. Never in a million years could he have imagined this possibility...

He'd assumed that the stressful times when he and Ellie had tried for a family were well and truly behind him.

Since he'd left Karinya Station, he hadn't allowed himself to give a single thought to those few remaining embryos. How many were there? Two? Three?

A heavy weight pressed against his ribs now as he

remembered the painful stretch of years when the IVF clinic had dominated his and Ellie's lives. All their hopes and dreams had been pinned on the embryos. They'd even had a nickname for them.

Their *sproglets*.

So far, none of them had survived implantation…

The ordeal had been beyond heartbreaking.

Now… Joe had no doubt that Ellie was setting herself up for another round of bitter disappointment. And yet, for a crazy moment he almost felt hope flare inside him, the same hope that had skyrocketed and plunged and kept them on edge through those bleak years of trying.

Even now, Joe couldn't help feeling hopeful for Ellie's sake, although he knew that her chances of a successful pregnancy were slimmer than a hair's breadth. And it stung him to know that she planned to go ahead this time on her own.

Truth was, he didn't want to think about this. Not any aspect of it. He'd joined the Army to forget his stuffed-up life. Here, he had a visible, assailable enemy to keep him focused day and night.

Now Ellie was forcing him to once again contemplate fatherhood and all its responsibilities. Except, this time, it would be fatherhood in name only. She'd made it very clear that she still wanted the divorce, and Joe totally understood why. So even if there was an against-all-the-odds miracle and he found himself technically a father, his kid would never grow up under his roof.

They would be more or less strangers.

Almost as an accompaniment to this grim thought, an explosion sounded outside, too close for comfort. Through the hut's window Joe saw bright flashes and smoke, heard frantic voices calling. Another rocket-propelled grenade had dumped—a timely reminder that danger and death were his regular companions.

There was no escaping that and, if he was honest, there was absolutely no point in going over and over this question of Ellie's. It was a waste of time weighing up the pros and cons of his wife's request.

Already Joe knew his answer. It was a clear no-brainer.

CHAPTER ONE

Three years later...

'ELLIE, IT'S MUM. Do you have the television on?'

'Television?' Ellie's response was incredulous. 'Mum, I've just come in from the paddocks. Our dams are drying out. I've been wrestling with a bogged cow all afternoon and I'm covered in mud. Why? What's on TV?' The only show that interested Ellie these days was the weather.

'I just saw Joe,' her mother said.

Ellie gasped. 'On TV?'

'Yes, darling. On the news.'

'He...he hasn't been hurt?'

'No, no, he's fine.' There was a dismissive note in her mother's voice, a familiar reminder that she'd never approved of her daughter's choice of husband and that, eventually, she'd been proved right. 'You know he's home for good this time?'

'He's already back in Australia?'

'Yes, Ellie. His regiment or squadron or whatever it's called has just landed in Sydney. I caught it on the early news, and there was a glimpse of Joe. Only a few seconds, mind you, but it was definitely him. And the reporter's saying these troops won't be going back to Afghanistan. I thought you should know.'

'OK. Thanks.' Ellie pressed a hand to her chest, caught out by the unexpected thud of her heart.

'You might be able to catch the story on one of the other channels.'

'Yes, I guess.'

Ellie was trembling as she hung up. Of course she'd heard the news reports about a staged withdrawal of Australian troops, but it was still a shock to know that Joe was already home. For good this time.

As a Commando, Joe had been on dozens of short-term missions to Afghanistan, returning each time to his Army base down in New South Wales. But now he wouldn't be going back.

And yet he hadn't made any kind of contact.

It showed how very far apart they'd drifted.

Almost fearfully, Ellie glanced at the silent blank TV screen in the corner of the homestead lounge room. She didn't really have time to turn it on. She was disgustingly muddy after her tussle in the dam with the bogged cow and she needed to get out of these stinking clothes. She wasn't even sure why she'd rushed inside to answer the phone in this filthy state, but some instinct had sent her running.

She should get changed and showered before she did anything else. She wouldn't even look for Nina and Jacko until she was clean.

But, even as she told herself what she *should* do, Ellie picked up the remote. More than one channel would cover the return.

It took a few seconds of scrolling before she found a

scene at Mascot Airport and a journalist's voiceover reporting an emotional welcome for the returning troops.

The screen showed the airport crowded with soldiers in uniform, hugging their wives and lifting their children high, their tanned, lean faces lit by unmistakable excitement and emotion.

Tears and happy smiles abounded. A grinning young man was awkwardly holding a tiny baby. A little girl hugged her daddy's khaki-clad knee, trying to catch his attention while he kissed her mother.

Ellie's throat ached. The scene was crammed with images of family joy. Tears pricked her eyes and she wondered where Joe was.

And then she saw him.

The man who would soon be her ex.

At the back of the crowd. Grim-faced. He was skirting the scenes of elated families, as if he was trying to keep out of camera range while he made his way purposefully to the exit.

He looked so alone.

With his green Commando's beret set rakishly on his short dark hair, Joe looked so tall and soldierly. Handsome, of course. But, compared with his laughing, happy comrades, he also looked very severe. And so *very* alone.

Ellie's mouth twisted out of shape. Tears spilled. She didn't know why—she simply couldn't help it.

Then the camera shifted to a politician who'd arrived to welcome the troops.

Quickly, she snapped the remote and the images vanished.

She let out her breath in a despairing huff. She felt

shaken at seeing Joe again after so long. To her dismay, it had been more like a horse kick to her heart.

She drew a deeper calming breath, knowing she had to set unhelpful sentimentality aside. She'd been braced for Joe's return and she'd known what was required.

Their divorce would be finalised now and it was time to be sensible and stoic. She knew very well there was *no* prospect of a happy reunion. She and Joe had made each other too miserable for too long. If she was honest, she wasn't surprised that Joe hadn't bothered to tell her his deployment was over. She didn't mind really.

But she *did* mind that he hadn't even asked to see Jacko.

Joe stood at the motel window on Sydney's Coogee Beach, looking out at an idyllic moonlit scene of sea cliffs and rolling surf.

So, it was over. He was home—finally, permanently. On the long flight back from Afghanistan he'd been dreaming of this arrival.

For most Australians, December meant the beginning of the long summer holidays and Joe had looked forward to downing a cold beer at sunset in a bar overlooking the beach, and sitting on the sand, eating hot, crunchy fish and chips straight from the paper they were wrapped in, throwing the scraps to the seagulls.

This evening he'd done all of these things, but the expected sense of joy and relaxation hadn't followed. Everything had felt strangely unreal.

It was unsettling, especially as his Commando training had taught him to adapt quickly to different environments and to respond effectively to any challenges.

Now he was home, in the safest and most welcoming

of environments, and yet he felt detached and disconnected, as if he was standing on the outside, watching some stranger trying to enjoy himself.

Of course, he knew that the transition to civilian life would be tricky after years of strict training and dangerous combat. At least he'd been prepared for the Happy Family scenes at the airport today, but once he'd escaped those jubilant reunions he'd expected to be fine.

Instead he felt numb and deflated, as if nothing about this new life was real.

He stared at the crescent of pale sand below, silvery in the moonlight, at the rolling breakers and white foam spraying against the dark, rocky cliffs, and he half-wished he had new orders to obey and a dangerous mission to fulfil.

When his phone buzzed, he didn't have the heart to answer it but, out of habit, he checked the caller ID.

It was Ellie.

His gut tightened.

He hadn't expected her to call so soon, but perhaps she'd seen the TV news and she knew he was back in Sydney. No doubt she wanted to talk, to make arrangements.

His breathing went shallow as hope and dread warred inside him. Was he ready for this conversation?

It was tempting to let her call go through to voice-mail, to see what she had to say and respond later. But in the last half-second he gave in. He swallowed to clear his throat. 'Hi, Ellie.'

'Oh? Hello, Joe.'

They'd spoken a handful of times in the past three years.

'How are you?' Joe grimaced, knowing how awkward he sounded. 'How's the kid?'

'We're both really well, thanks. Jacko's growing so fast. How are you?'

What could he say? 'Fine. Home in one piece.'

'It must be wonderful to be back in Australia for good,' she said warmly.

'Yeah, I guess.' Too late he realised he should have sounded more enthusiastic.

'I...ah...' Now, it was Ellie who seemed to be floundering for words.

They weren't good at this. How could they be? An unhappy silence ticked by.

'I hear you've had a very dry year up north,' Joe said, clumsily picking up the ball.

'We have, but the weather bureau's predicting a decent wet season.'

'Well, that's good news.'

Joe pictured Karinya, the Far North Queensland cattle station that he and Ellie had leased and set up together when they'd first been married and afloat on love and hope and a thousand happy dreams. In his mind's eye, he could see the red dirt of the inland and the pale, sparse grass dotted with cattle, the rocky ridges and winding creeks. The wide blue overarching sky.

When they'd split, Ellie had stubbornly insisted on staying up there and running the place on her own. Even when the much-longed-for baby had arrived she'd stayed on, hiring a manager at first while she was pregnant, and then a nanny to help with the baby while Ellie continued to look after the cattle business as well as her son.

His son. Their son.

'Joe, I assume you want to see Jacko,' Ellie said quickly.

He gritted his teeth against the sudden whack of emotion. There'd been opportunities to visit North Queensland between his many missions, but he'd only seen their miracle baby once. He'd flown to Townsville and Ellie had driven in to the coast from Karinya. They'd spent an awkward afternoon in a park on Townsville's Strand and Joe had a photo in his wallet to prove it.

Now the kid was two years old.

'Of course I'd like to see Jacko,' he said cautiously. How could a father not want to see his own son? 'Are you planning to come in to Townsville again?'

'I'm sorry, Joe, I can't. It's more or less impossible for me to get away just now. You know what it's like in December. It's calving time, and I'm busy with keeping supplements and water up to the herd. And Nina— that's the nanny—wants to take her holidays. She'd like to go home to Cairns for Christmas, and that's understandable, so I'm trying to manage here on my own. I…um…thought you might be able to come out here.'

Joe's jaw tightened. 'To the homestead?'

'Yes.'

His brow furrowed. 'But even if I fly to Townsville, I wouldn't be able to make it out to Karinya and back again in a day.'

'Yes, I know…you'd have to stay overnight. There… there's a spare bed. You could have Nina's room.'

Whoa.

Joe flinched as if he'd been hit by a sniper. He held the phone away at arm's length as he dragged a shaky breath. He'd been steeling himself for the heart slug of another meeting with his son, but he'd always imagined another half hour in Townsville—a handover of gifts, maybe a walk in the park and another photo of himself with the kid, a memory to treasure.

Get it over, and then goodbye.

He wasn't sure he was prepared to stay at Karinya, spending all that time with young Jacko, as Ellie called him, spending a night there as well.

That had to be a bad idea.

Crazy.

'Joe, are you still there?'

'Yeah.' The effort to sound cool and calm made him grimace. 'Ellie, I'm not sure about going out there.'

'What do you mean? You *do* want to see your little boy, don't you?'

The hurt in her voice was crystal freaking clear.

'I…I do… Sure, of course I want to see him.'

'I thought you'd want to at least give him a Christmas present, Joe. He's old enough now to understand about presents.'

Joe sighed.

'But if you'd rather not…' Her voice was frosty now, reminding him of the chill factor that had caused him so much angst in the past.

'Look, I just got back. I'm jet-lagged, and there's all kinds of stuff to sort out here.' It wasn't totally the truth and Ellie probably guessed he was stalling.

'You and I have things to sort out, too.'

Joe drew a sharp breath. 'Do you have the papers from the solicitor?'

'All ready and waiting.'

'OK.' He felt the cold steel of a knife at his throat. 'Can I call you in the morning?'

By then he'd hopefully have his head together.

'Sure, Joe. Whatever.' Again, he heard the iciness that had plunged their once burning passion to below freezing point.

'Thanks for the call, Ellie.' With an effort he managed to sound non-combative, aware they were already falling into the old patterns that had eroded their marriage—constantly upsetting each other and then trying to placate, and then upsetting each other yet again. 'And thanks for the invitation.'

'No worries,' she said, sounding very worried indeed.

Damn him!

Ellie stood beside the phone, arms tightly crossed, trying to hold herself together, determined she wouldn't allow her disappointment to spill over into tears. She'd shed enough tears over Joe Madden to last two lifetimes.

It had taken considerable courage to ring him. She was proud she'd made the first move. But what had she expected? Warmth and delight from Joe?

What a fool she could be.

If Joe came to Karinya, it would be to sign the papers and nothing more. He would be businesslike and distant with her and with Jacko. How on earth had she once fallen for such a cold man?

Blinking and swiping at her eyes, Ellie walked softly through the house to the door to Jacko's room. Her little boy slept with a night light—an orange turtle with a purple and green spotted bow tie—and in the light's glow she could see the golden sheen of his hair, the soft downy curve of his baby-plump cheek.

He looked small and vulnerable when he was asleep, but in the daytime he was a ball of energy, usually good-natured and sunny, and gleefully eager to embrace life—the life he'd been granted so miraculously.

Ellie knew Joe would melt when he saw him. Surely?

Perhaps Joe sensed this possibility. Perhaps he was afraid?

Actually, that was probably close to the truth. The Joe Madden she remembered would rather face a dangerous enemy intent on death and destruction than deal with his deepest emotions.

Ellie sighed. This next phase of her life wasn't going to be easy, but she was determined to be strong while she and Joe sorted out the ground rules for their future. The impending divorce had been hanging over them for years like an axe waiting to fall. Now, she just wanted it to be over. Finalised.

But she planned to handle the arrangements with dignity and good sense, and she aimed to be mature and evolved in all her dealings with Joe.

It probably helped that they were more or less strangers now.

This was a bad idea. Crazy.

The more Joe paced in his motel room, the more he was sure that going back to the homestead was a risk he didn't want to take. Of course he was curious to see his son, but he'd always anticipated that his final meeting with Ellie would be in a lawyer's office. Somewhere neutral, without memories attached.

Going back to Karinya was bound to be painful, for a thousand different reasons.

He had to remember all the sane and sensible reasons why he'd suggested the divorce, beginning with the guilty knowledge that he'd more or less trapped Ellie into marriage in the first place.

The unexpected pregnancy, their hasty marriage followed by a miscarriage and a host of fertility issues.

Now, since Jacko's arrival, the goalposts had shifted, but Joe had no illusions about a reconciliation with Ellie. After four years in the Army, he was a hardened realist and he'd seen too much injury and death to believe in second chances.

Of course, today hadn't been the only time Joe had landed back in Australia to find himself the sole father in his unit with no family to greet him. He was used to seeing his mates going home with their wives and kids, knowing they were sharing meals and laughter, knowing they were making love to their wives, while he paced in an empty motel room.

Until today, his return visits had always been temporary, a short spot of leave before he was back in action. This time, it was unsettling to know he wouldn't be going back to war. His four years of service were over.

Yeah, of course he was lucky to still be alive and uninjured. And yet, tonight, after one phone conversation with Ellie, Joe didn't want to put a name to how he felt, but it certainly wasn't any version of lucky.

Of course, if he hadn't been so hung up on leaving a widow's pension for her, they would have been divorced years ago when they'd first recognised that their marriage was unsalvageable. They could have made a clean break then, and by now he would have well and truly adjusted to his single status.

Almost certainly, there wouldn't have been a cute complication named Jackson Joseph Madden.

Jacko.

Joe let out his breath on a sigh, remembering his excitement on the day the news of his son's birth came through. It had been such a miracle! He'd even broken his habitual silence about his personal life and had made an announcement in the mess. There'd been cheering and table-thumping and back slaps, and he'd passed his phone around with the photos that Ellie had sent of a tiny red-faced baby boy wrapped in a blue and white blanket.

He'd almost felt like a regular proud and happy new father.

Later, on leave, when his mates quizzed him about Ellie and Jacko, he was able to use the vast distance between the Holsworthy Base and their Far North Queensland cattle station as a valid excuse for his family's absence.

Now that excuse no longer held.

He and Ellie had to meet and sign the blasted papers. He supposed it made sense to travel up to Karinya straight away.

It wouldn't be a picnic, though, seeing Ellie again and looking around the property they'd planned to run together, not to mention going through another meeting with the son he would not help Ellie to raise.

And, afterwards, Joe would be expected to go home to his family's cattle property in Central Queensland, where his mother would smother him with sympathy and ply him with questions about the boy.

As an added hurdle, Christmas was looming just around the corner, bringing with it a host of emotional trapdoors.

Surely coming home should be easier than this?

CHAPTER TWO

WHEN ELLIE'S PHONE rang early next morning, Jacko was refusing to eat his porridge and he was banging his spoon on his high chair's tray, demanding. 'Eggie,' at the top of his voice.

For weeks now, Nina, the nanny, had supervised Jacko's breakfast while Ellie was out at the crack of dawn, delivering supplements to the cattle and checking on the newborn calves and their mothers.

Now Nina was in Cairns with her family for Christmas and as the phone trilled, Ellie shot a despairing glance to the rooster-shaped kitchen wall clock. No one she knew would call at this early hour.

Jacko shrieked again for his boiled egg.

Ellie was already in a bad mood when she answered. 'Hello? This is Karinya.'

'Good morning.' It was Joe, sounding gruff and businesslike. Very military.

'Good morning, Joe.' Behind Ellie, Jacko wailed, 'Eggie,' more loudly than ever.

'Would Friday suit?'

She frowned. Did Joe have to be so clipped and cryptic? 'To come here?'

'Yes.'

Friday was only the day after tomorrow. It wasn't much warning. Ellie's heart began an unhelpful drumming, followed by a flash of heat, as if her body had a mind of its own, as if it was remembering, without her permission, the fireworks Joe used to rouse in her. His kisses, his touch, the sparks a single look from him could light.

In the early days of their marriage, they hadn't been able to keep their hands off each other. Back in the heady days before everything went wrong, before their relationship exploded into a thousand painful pieces.

'I could catch a flight that arrives in Townsville around eight a.m.,' Joe said. 'If I hire a car, I could probably get to Karinya around mid-afternoon.'

'Eggie!' Jacko bawled in a fully-fledged bellow.

'Is that the kid crying?'

His name's Jacko, Ellie wanted to remind Joe. Why did he have to call him 'the kid'?

Holding the receiver to one ear, she filled a cup with juice and handed it to Jacko, hoping it would calm him. 'He's waiting for his breakfast.'

Jacko accepted the juice somewhat disconsolately, and at last the room was blessedly silent.

'So how about Friday?' Joe asked again.

At the thought of seeing him in less than forty-eight hours, Ellie took a deep, very necessary breath. 'Friday will be fine.'

It would *have* to be fine. They *had* to do this. They had to get it over and behind them. Only then could they both finally move on.

Joe was an hour away from Karinya when he noticed the gathering clouds. The journey had taken him west from Townsville to Charters Towers and then north through Queensland's more remote cattle country. It was an unhappily nostalgic drive, over familiar long, straight roads and sweeping open country, broken by occasional rocky ridges or the sandy dip of a dry creek bed.

The red earth and pale, drought-bleached grass were dotted with cattle and clumps of acacia and ironbark trees. It was a landscape Joe knew as well as his own reflection, but he'd rarely allowed himself to think about it since he'd left Queensland five and a half years ago.

Now, he worked hard to block out the memories of his life here with Ellie. And yet every signpost and landmark seemed to trigger an unstoppable flow.

He was reliving the day he and Ellie had first travelled up here, driving up from Ridgelands in his old battered ute. No one else in either of their families had ventured this far north, and the journey had felt like an adventure, as if they were pioneers pushing into new frontiers.

He remembered their first sight of Karinya—coming over a rise and seeing the simple iron-roofed homestead set in the middle of grassy plains. On the day they'd signed up for the long-term lease they'd been buzzing with excitement.

On the day their furniture arrived, Ellie had raced around like an enthusiastic kid. She'd wanted to help shift the furniture, but of course Joe wouldn't let her. She was pregnant, after all. So she'd unpacked boxes and filled cupboards. She'd made up their bed and she'd scrubbed the bathroom and the kitchen, even though they'd been perfectly clean.

She'd baked a roast dinner, which was a bit burnt,

but they'd laughed about it and picked off the black bits. And Ellie had been *incredibly* happy, as if their simple house in the middle of hundreds of empty acres represented a long and cherished dream that had finally come true.

When they made love on that first night it was as if being in their new bed, in their new home, had brought them a new level of connection and closeness they hadn't dreamed was possible.

Afterwards they'd lain close and together they'd watched the stars outside through the as yet uncurtained bedroom window.

Joe had seen a shooting star. 'Look!' he'd said, sitting up quickly. 'Did you see it?'

'Yes!' Ellie's eyes were shining.

'We should make a wish,' he said and, almost without thinking, he wished that they could always be as happy as they were on this night.

Ellie, however, was frowning. 'Have you made your wish?' she asked.

'Yes.' He smiled at her. 'What about you?'

'No, I haven't. I…I don't know if I want to.' She sounded perplexingly frightened. 'I…I don't really like making wishes. It's too much like tempting fate.'

Surprised, Joe laughed at her fears. He ran a gentle hand down her arm and lightly touched her stomach, where their tiny baby lay.

'Do *you* think I should make a wish?' Ellie's expression was serious now.

'Sure.' Joe was on top of the world that night. 'What harm can it do?'

She smiled and nestled into his embrace. 'OK. I wish for a boy. A cute little version of you.'

Three weeks later, Ellie had a miscarriage.

Remembering, Joe let out an involuntary sigh. *Enough.*

Don't go there.

He forced his attention back to the country stretching away to the horizon on either side of the road. Having grown up on a cattle property, he was able to assess the condition of the cattle he passed and the scant remaining fodder. There was no question that the country needed rain.

Everywhere, he saw signs of drought and stress. Although Ellie would have employed contract fencers and ringers for mustering, she must have worked like a demon to keep up with the demands of the prolonged drought.

He found himself questioning, as he had many times, why she'd been so stubbornly determined to stay out here. Alone.

He stopped for bad coffee and a greasy hamburger in a tiny isolated Outback servo, and it was only when he came outside again that he saw the dark clouds gathering on the northern horizon. Too often in December, clouds like these merely taunted graziers without bringing rain, but, as he drove on, drawing closer to Karinya, the clouds closed in.

Within thirty minutes the clouds covered the entire spread of the sky, hovering low to the earth like a cotton wool dressing pressed down over a wound.

As Joe turned off the main road and rattled over the cattle grid onto the track that led to the homestead, the first heavy drops began to fall, splattering the hire vehicle's dusty windscreen. By the time he reached the house the rain was pelting down.

To his faint surprise, Ellie was on the front veranda, waiting for him. She was wearing an Akubra hat and a Drizabone coat over jeans but, despite the masculine gear, she looked as slim and girlish as ever.

She had another coat over her arm and she hurried down the front steps, holding it out to him. Peering through the heavy curtain of rain, Joe saw unmistakable worry in her dark brown eyes.

'Here,' she yelled, raising her voice above the thundering noise on the homestead's iron roof, and as soon as he opened the driver's door, she shoved the coat through the chink.

A moment later, he was out of the vehicle, with the coat over his head, and the two of them were dashing through the rain and up the steps.

'This is incredible, isn't it?' Ellie gasped as they reached the veranda. 'Such lousy timing.' She turned to Joe. Beneath the dripping brim of her hat, her dark eyes were wide with concern.

He wondered if he was the cause.

'Have you heard the weather report?' she asked.

He shook his head. 'Not a word. I haven't had the radio on. Why? What's happening?'

'A cyclone. Cyclone Peta. It started up in the Gulf yesterday afternoon, and crossed the coast mid-morning. It's dumping masses of rain further north.'

'I guess that's good news.'

'Well, yes, it is. We certainly need the rain.' She frowned. 'But I have a paddock full of cattle down by the river.'

'The Hopkins paddock,' Joe said, remembering the section of their land that had flooded nearly every wet season.

Ellie nodded.

'We need to get them out of there,' he said.

'I know.' Her soft pink mouth twisted into an apologetic wincing smile. 'Joe, I hate to do this to you when you've just arrived, but you know how quickly these rivers can rise. I'd like to shift the cattle this afternoon. Now, actually.'

'OK. Let's get going, then.'

'You don't mind?'

''Course I don't.' In truth, he was relieved to have something practical to do. A mission to rescue cattle was a darn sight more appealing than sitting around drinking tea and trying to make polite conversation with his beautiful soon-to-be ex.

'It's flat country, so we won't need horses. I'll have to take Jacko, though, so I thought I'd take the ute with the trail bike in the back.'

Joe nodded.

'One problem. I'd probably have to stay in the ute with Jacko.' Ellie swallowed, as if she was nervous. 'Would you mind…um…looking after the round-up?'

'Sure. Sounds like a plan.' He chanced a quick smile. 'As long as I haven't lost my touch.'

As he said this, Ellie stared at him for longer than necessary, her expression slightly puzzled and questioning. She opened her mouth as if she was going to say something in response, but then she shook her head as if she'd changed her mind.

'I'll get Jacko. He's having an afternoon nap.' She shrugged out of her coat and beneath it she was wearing a neat blue and white striped shirt tucked into jeans. Her waistline was still as trim as a schoolgirl's.

When she took off her hat, Joe's gaze fixed on her

thick dark hair, pulled back into a glossy braid. Her hair had always been soft to touch despite its thickness.

'Come on in,' she said awkwardly over her shoulder. 'You don't mind if we leave your gear in your car until later?'

He shrugged. 'It's only Christmas presents.'

'Would you...ah...like a cup of tea or anything?'

'No, I'm fine.' The muddy coffee he'd had on the road would take a while to digest. 'Let's collect the kid and get this job done.'

They took off their boots and hung their wet coats on the row of pegs that Joe had mounted beside the front door when they'd first moved in here. To his surprise, his own battered elderly Akubra still hung on the end peg.

Of course, he'd known it would feel strange to follow Ellie into the house as her guest rather than her partner, but the knife thrust in his gut was an unpleasant addition.

The house was full of the furniture they'd chosen together in Townsville—the tan leather sofa and the oval dining table, the rocking chair Ellie had insisted on buying when she was first pregnant.

Joe wouldn't take a stick of this furniture when they divorced. He was striking new trails.

'I'll fetch Jacko,' Ellie said nervously. 'I reckon he'll be awake by now.'

Unsure if he was expected to follow her, Joe remained standing, almost to attention, in the centre of the lounge room. He heard the creak of a floorboard down the hall and the soft warmth in Ellie's voice as she greeted their son. Then he heard the boy's happy crow of delight.

'Mummy, Mummy!'

Joe felt his heart twist.

Moments later, Ellie appeared in the doorway with Jacko in her arms. The boy was a sturdy little fellow, with glowing blue eyes and cheeks still pink and flushed with sleep. He was cuteness personified. Very blond— Joe had been blond until he was six and then his hair had turned dark.

The last time Joe had seen his son, he'd been a sleepy baby, barely able to hold his head up. Now he was a little man.

And he and Ellie were a winsome pair. Joe couldn't help noticing how happy Ellie looked now, with an extra aura of softness and womanly warmth about her that made her lovelier than ever.

She was complete now, he decided. She had what she'd so badly wanted, and he was truly happy for her. Perhaps it was fitting that this miracle had only occurred after Joe had stepped out of the picture.

Jacko was grinning at him. 'Man!' he announced in noisy delight.

'This is Joe,' Ellie told him, her voice a tad shaky. 'You can say *Joe*, can't you, big boy?'

'Joe!' the boy echoed with a triumphant grin.

'So he's going to call me Joe? Not Dad?'

Ellie frowned as if he'd let fly with a swear word.

'You've been away,' she said tightly. 'And you're going away again. Jacko's only two, and if you're not going to be around us he can't be expected to understand the concept of a father. Calling you Daddy would only confuse him.'

Joe's teeth clenched. He almost demanded to know

if she had another guy already waiting in the wings. A stepfather?

'Jacko's bound to understand about fathers eventually,' he said tersely.

'And we'll face that explanation when the time is right.' A battle light glowed in Ellie's dark eyes.

Damn it, they were at it already. Joe gave a carefully exaggerated shrug. *Whatever.* He'd had enough of war at home *and* abroad. On this visit he was determined to remain peaceful.

He turned his attention to his son. 'So how are you, Jacko?'

The boy squirmed and held out his arms. 'Down,' he demanded. 'I want Man.'

With an anxious smile, Ellie released him.

The little boy rushed at Joe's legs and looked up at him with big blue eyes and a grin of triumph.

What now? Joe thought awkwardly. He reached down and took his son's tiny plump hand and gave it a shake. 'Pleased to meet you, Jacko.'

He deliberately avoided noting Ellie's reaction.

They drove down to the river flats with their son strapped into the toddler seat between them, and Ellie tried not to mind that Jacko seemed to be obsessed with Joe.

The whole way, the little boy kept giggling and making eyes at the tall dark figure beside him, and he squealed with delight when Joe pulled faces.

A man's presence at Karinya was a novelty, of course, and Ellie knew that Jacko had been starved of masculine company. He was always intrigued by any male visitor.

Problem was that today Ellie was almost as intrigued as her son, especially when she watched Joe take off on the trail bike through the rain and the mud. He looked so spectacularly athletic and fit and so totally at home on the back of a motorbike, rounding up the herd, ducking and weaving through patches of scrub.

He certainly hadn't lost his touch.

'Show-off,' she muttered with a reluctant grim smile as he jumped the bike over a pile of fallen timber and then skilfully edged the stragglers forward into the mob, heading them up the slope towards the open gate where she was parked.

'Joe!' Jacko cried, bouncing in his car seat and pointing through the windscreen. He clapped his hands. 'Look, Mummy! Joe!'

'Yeah, he looks good, all right,' Ellie had to admit. In terms of skill and getting the job done quickly, Joe might never have been away.

And that felt dangerous.

Out of the blue, she found herself remembering their wedding day and the short ceremony in the register office in Townsville. She and Joe had decided they didn't want to go through awkward explanations about her pregnancy to their families, and neither of them had wanted the fuss of a big family wedding.

They'd both agreed they could deal with their families later. On that day, all they'd wanted was to commit to each other. Their elopement had seemed *soooo* romantic.

But it had also been reckless, Ellie thought now as she saw how brightly her son's eyes shone as he watched Joe.

'Don't be too impressed, sweetheart. Take Mummy's word; it's simply not worth it. That man will only break your heart.'

Jacko merely chortled.

It was dark by the time Joe came into the kitchen, having showered and changed into dry clothes. Outside, the rain still pelted down, drumming on the roof and streaming over the edge of the guttering, but Ellie had closed the French windows leading onto the veranda and the kitchen was bright and cosy.

She tried not to notice how red-hot attractive Joe looked in a simple white T-shirt and blue jeans, with his dark hair damp from the shower, his bright eyes an unforgettable piercing blue. The man was still unlawfully sexy.

But Joe seemed to have acquired a lone wolf aura now. In addition to his imperfect nose that had been broken in a punch-up when he was seventeen, there was a hard don't-mess-with-me look in his eyes that made her wonder what he'd been through over the past four years.

Almost certainly, he'd been required to kill people, and she couldn't quite get her head around that. How had that changed him?

The Army had kept the Commandos' deployments short and frequent in a bid to minimise post-traumatic stress, but no soldier returned from war unscarred. These days, everyone knew that. For Ellie, there was the extra, heavily weighing knowledge that their unhappy marriage had pushed Joe in the Army's direction.

And now, here they were, standing in the same room, but she was painfully aware of the wide, unbridgeable chasm that gaped open between them.

She turned and lifted the lid on the slow cooker, giving its contents a stir, wishing she was more on top of this situation.

'That smells amazing,' said Joe.

She felt a small flush of satisfaction. She'd actually set their dinner simmering earlier in the day, hoping it would fill the kitchen with enticing aromas, but she responded to Joe's compliment with a casual shrug and tried not to look too pleased. 'It's just a Spanish chicken dish.'

'Spanish?' Joe raised a quizzical eyebrow.

No doubt he was remembering her previously limited range of menus. 'I've broadened my recipe repertoire.'

Joe almost smiled, but then he seemed to change his mind. Sinking his hands into his jeans pockets, he looked around the kitchen, taking in the table set with red and white gingham mats and the sparkling white cupboards and timber bench tops. 'You've also been decorating.'

Ellie nodded. 'Before I became pregnant with Jacko I painted just about every wall and cupboard in the house.'

'The nesting instinct?'

'Something like that.'

Joe frowned at this, his eyes taking on an ambiguous gleam as he stared hard at the cupboards. His Adam's apple jerked in his throat. 'It looks great,' he said gruffly.

But Ellie felt suddenly upset. It felt wrong to be showing off her homemaker skills when she had absolutely no plans to share this home with him.

'Where's Jacko?' he asked, abruptly changing the subject

'Watching TV. Nina's recorded his favourite programmes, and he's happy to watch them over and over. It helps him to wind down at the end of the day.'

This was met by a slow nod but, instead of wandering off to check out his son, Joe continued to stand in the middle of the kitchen with his hands in his pockets, his gaze thoughtful.

'He doesn't watch a lot of TV,' Ellie felt compelled to explain. 'I...I usually read him story books as well.'

'I'm sure he loves that.' Joe's blue eyes blazed. 'Chill, Ellie. I'm not here to judge you. I'm sure you're a great mum. Fantastic.'

Her smile wobbled uncertainly. Why would this compliment make her want to cry?

They should try to relax. She should offer Joe a pre-dinner beer or a glass of wine.

But, before she could suggest this, he said, 'So, I guess this is as good a time as any for me to sign those divorce papers?'

Ellie's stomach dropped as if she'd fallen from the top of a mountain. 'Well...um...yes,' she said, but she had to grip the bench behind her before her knees gave way. 'You could sign now...or after dinner.'

'It's probably best to get it over with and out of the way.'

'I guess.' Her reply was barely a whisper. It was ridiculous. She'd been waiting for this moment for so long. They'd arranged an out of court settlement and their future plans were clear—she would keep on with the lease at Karinya, and Joe had full access to Jacko, although she wasn't sure how often he planned to see his son.

This settlement was what she wanted, of course, and

yet she felt suddenly bereft, as if a great hole had opened up in her life, almost as if someone had died.

What on earth was the matter with her? Joe's signature would provide her with her ticket of leave.

Freedom beckoned.

The feeling of loss was nothing more than a temporary lapse, an aberration brought on by the unscheduled spot of cattle work that she and Joe had shared this afternoon. Rounding up the herd by the river had felt too dangerously like the good old days when they'd still been in love.

'Ellie?' Joe was standing stiffly to attention now, his eyes alert but cool, watching her intently. 'You're OK about this, aren't you?'

'Yes, of course. I'm totally fine.' She spoke quickly, not quite meeting his gaze, and then she drew a deep, fortifying breath, hoping it would stop the trembling in her knees. 'The papers are in the study.'

'Ellie.'

The unexpected gentleness in his voice brought her spinning around. 'Yes?'

'I wish…'

'What?' She almost snapped this question.

What do you wish? Tell me quickly, Joe.

Did he wish they didn't have to do this? Was he asking for another chance to save their marriage?

'I wish you didn't look so pale and upset.'

Her attempt to laugh came out as a hiccup. Horrified, she seized on the handiest weapon—anger. It was the weapon she'd used so often with this man, firing holes into the bedrock of their marriage. 'If I'm upset, Joe, it's because this is a weird situation.'

'But we agreed.' He seemed angry, too, but his anger

was annoyingly cold and controlled. 'It's what you want, isn't it?'

'Sure, we agreed, and yes, it's what I want. But it's still weird. How many people agree to a divorce and then put it on hold for four years?'

'You know why we did that—so you'd be looked after financially if I was killed.'

'Yes, I know, and that was generous of you. Just the same, it hasn't been a picnic here.' Suddenly, Ellie could feel the long months of tension giving way inside her, rushing to the surface, hot and explosive. 'While you were away being the hero in Afghanistan, you were distracted by everything over there. But I was *here*, supposed to be divorced, but surrounded by all of this.'

Flinging her arm dramatically, she gestured to the homestead and the paddocks beyond. 'Every day, I was left with the remnants of our lives together. A constant reminder of everything that went wrong.'

'So why did you stay?' Joe asked coolly.

Ellie gasped, momentarily caught out. 'I'm surprised you have to ask,' she said quickly to cover her confusion.

He shrugged a cool, questioning eyebrow.

And Ellie looked away. She'd asked herself the same question often enough. She knew exactly why she'd stayed. Even now, she could hear her dad's voice from all those years ago. *If you start something, Ellie, you've got to see it through.*

Her dad had told her this just before her thirteenth birthday. She'd been promised a horse for her birthday and he'd been building proper stables instead of the old two-sided tin shelter they'd had until then.

Ellie had helped him by holding hammers or the long

pieces of timber and she'd handed up nails and screws. While they worked her dad had reminded her that owning a horse was a long-term project.

'You can't take up a responsibility like a horse and then lose interest,' he'd said. 'I've known people like that. They never stick at anything, always have to be trying something different, and they end up unhappy and wondering what went wrong.'

Tragically, her father had never finished those stables. He'd also he'd been mending a windmill and he'd fallen and died three days before Ellie's birthday. In the bleak months that followed, Ellie's mum had sold their farm and moved into town, and the horse that should have been Ellie's had gone to another girl in her class at school.

In a matter of months, Ellie lost everything—her darling father, her beloved farm, her dreams of owning a horse. And the bittersweet irony of her father's words had been seared into her brain.

If you start something, you've got to see it through.

Years later, with a failed marriage and failed attempts at parenthood weighing her down, she'd been determined that she wouldn't let go of Karinya as well.

'So why did you stay here?' Joe repeated.

With her arms folded protectively over her chest, Ellie told him. 'I love this place, Joe. I'm proud of it, and I've worked hard to improve it. It was hard enough giving up half a dream without giving up Karinya as well.'

Joe's only reaction was to stand very still, watching her with a stern, unreadable gaze. If Ellie hadn't been studying him with equal care, she might have missed the fleeting shadow that dimmed his bright blue eyes, or the telltale muscle twitching in his jaw.

But she did see these signs, and they made something unravel inside her.

Damn you, Joe. Tell me what you're thinking.

Painful seconds ticked by, but neither of them moved nor spoke. Ellie almost reached out and said, *Do we need to talk about this?*

But it wasn't an easy question to ask when it was Joe who'd originally suggested their divorce. He'd never shown any sign of backing down, so now her stubborn pride kept her silent.

Eventually, he said quietly, 'So, about this signing?'

Depressed but resolute, Ellie pointed to the doorway to the study. 'The papers are in here.'

As she reached the study, she didn't look back to check that Joe was following her. Skirting the big old silky oak desk that they'd bought at an antique shop in Charters Towers, she marched straight to the shelves Joe had erected all those years ago and she lifted down a well-thumbed Manila folder.

She sensed Joe behind her but she didn't look at him as she turned and placed the folder on the desk. In silence she opened it to reveal the sheaf of papers that she'd lodged with the courts.

'I guess you'll want to read these through,' she said, eyes downcast.

'There's no need. Geoffrey Bligh has sent me a copy. I know what it says.'

'Oh? All right.' Ellie opened a drawer and selected a black pen. 'So, I've served you with the papers, and all you need to do now is sign to acknowledge that you accept them.' She still couldn't look him in the eye.

She was trembling inside and she took a deep breath.

'There,' she said dully, setting the appropriate sheet

of paper on the desk and then stepping away to make room for Joe.

His face was stonily grim as he approached the desk, but he showed no sign of hesitation as he picked up the pen.

As he leaned over the desk, Ellie watched the neat dark line of his hair across the back of his neck and she saw a vein pulsing just below his ear. She noticed how strong his hand looked as he gripped the pen.

Unhelpfully, she remembered his hand, those fingers touching her when they made love. It seemed so long ago and yet it was so unforgettable.

There'd been a time in their marriage when they'd been so good at sex.

Joe scrawled his spiky signature, then set the pen down and stood staring fiercely at the page now decorated with his handwriting.

It was over.

In the morning he would take this final piece of paper with him to their solicitor but, to all intents and purposes, they were officially and irrevocably divorced.

And now they had to eat dinner together. Ellie feared the Spanish chicken would taste like dust in her mouth.

CHAPTER THREE

IT SHOULD HAVE been cosy eating Ellie's delicious meal in the homestead kitchen to the accompaniment of the steadily falling rain. But Joe had dined in Kabul when a car bomb exploded just outside and he'd felt more relaxed then than he did now with his ex.

It shouldn't be this way.

All their tensions were supposed to be behind them now. They were no longer man and wife. Their marriage was over, both in reality and on paper. It was like signing a peace treaty. No more disputes. Everything was settled.

They were free. Just friends. No added expectations.

And yet Ellie had barely touched the food she'd taken so much trouble to prepare. Joe supposed she wished he was gone—completely out of her hair.

As long as he hung around this place, they would both be besieged by this edgy awareness of each other that kept them on tenterhooks.

Ellie was meticulously shredding the tender chicken on her plate with her fork. 'So what are your plans now?' she asked in the carefully polite tone people used when they were making an effort to maintain a semblance of normality. 'Are you staying in the Army?'

Joe shook his head. 'I have a job lined up—with a government team in the Southern Ocean—patrolling for poachers and illegal fishermen.'

'The Southern Ocean?' Ellie couldn't have looked more surprised or upset if he'd announced he was going to mine asteroids in outer space. 'So...so Jacko won't see you at all?'

Annoyed by this, Joe shrugged. 'If you plan to stay out here, it wouldn't matter what sort of work I did—I still wouldn't be able to see the boy very often.'

'There's an Army base in Townsville.'

This was a surprise. He'd expected Ellie to be pleased that he'd be well away from her. 'As I said, I'm leaving the Army.'

Ellie's eyes widened. 'I thought you loved it. I thought it was supposed to be what you'd always wanted.'

'It was,' Joe said simply. For possibly the first time in his life, he'd felt a true sense of belonging with his fellow Commandos. He'd grown up as the youngest in his family, but he'd always been the little nuisance tagalong, hanging around his four older brothers, never quite big enough to keep up, never quite fitting in.

In the Army he'd truly discovered a 'band of brothers', united by the challenge and threat of active service. But everything about the Army would be different now, and he couldn't bear the thought of a desk job.

Ellie dipped her fork into a pile of savoury rice, but she didn't lift it to her mouth. 'I can't see you in a boat, rolling around in the Southern Ocean. You've always been a man of the land. You have all the bush skills and knowledge.'

It was true that Joe loved the bush, and he'd especially loved starting his own cattle business here at

Karinya. But what was the point of rehashing ancient history?

'I guess I feel like a change,' he said with a shrug.

'When do you have to start this new job?'

'In a few weeks. Mid-January.'

'That soon?'

He shrugged again. He was pleased he had an approaching deadline. Given the mess of his private life, he needed a plan, somewhere definite to go with new horizons.

'Will you mind—' Ellie began, but then she swallowed and looked away. 'Will it bother you that you won't see much of Jacko?'

Joe inhaled a sharp, instinctively protective breath. He was trying really hard not to think too much about his son, about all the milestones he'd already missed and those he would miss in the future—the day-to-day adventure of watching a small human being come to terms with the world. 'Maybe I'll be more use to him later on, when he's older.'

It was clearly the wrong thing to say.

Ellie's jaw jutted. She looked tenser than ever. Awkward seconds ticked by. Joe wished he didn't have to try so damn hard, even now, after they'd broken up.

'What about you?' he asked. 'I haven't asked how you are now. Are you keeping well?'

'I am well, actually. I think having Jacko has made a big difference, both mentally and physically. I must admit I'm a lot calmer these days. And I think all the hard outdoor work here has paid off as well.' She touched her stomach. 'Internally, things…um…seem to have settled down.'

'That's fantastic.' He knew how she'd suffered and he was genuinely pleased for her. 'So, do you have plans?'

'How do you mean?'

'Are you planning to move on from here?' Joe steeled himself. If there was a new man in her life, this was her chance to say so.

But her jaw dropped so hard Joe almost heard it crack.

'You're joking, aren't you?'

'Not at all.'

'You really think I could willingly leave Karinya?'

'Well, it's got to be tough for you out here on your own. You need help.'

'I hire help if I need it—fencing contractors, ringers, jillaroos...'

The relief he felt was ridiculous. He covered it with a casual shrug. 'I've heard it's hard to find workers these days. Everyone's heading for the mines.'

'I've managed.'

Joe couldn't resist prying. 'I suppose you might have a boyfriend lined up already?'

'Oh, for pity's sake.' Ellie was angry now.

And, although he knew it was foolish, he couldn't help having one last dig. 'I thought your mother might have had a victory. What was the name of that guy she picked out for you? The potato farmer near Hay? Orlando?'

'Roland,' Ellie said tightly. 'And he grows all sorts of vegetables—lettuce, pumpkins, tomatoes, corn—much more than potatoes. He's making a fortune, apparently.'

'Quite a catch,' Joe said, more coldly than he'd meant to.

'Yes, and a gentleman, too.' Ellie narrowed her eyes

at Joe. 'Do you really want me to give up this lease? Are you worried about the money?'

'No,' he snapped tersely. He couldn't deny he was impressed by Ellie's tenacity, even if it suggested that she was prepared to work much harder at the cattle business than she had at their marriage. 'I just think it's too big a property for a woman to run on her own, especially for a woman with a small child to care for as well.'

'Nina will be back after Christmas. She's great with Jacko.'

Joe recognised a brick wall when he ran into it and he let the subject drop. He suspected Ellie was as relieved as he was when the meal was finally over.

With the aid of night vision goggles, Joe made his way through a remote Afghan village, moving with the stealth of a panther on the prowl. In every dark alley and around every corner the threat of danger lurked and Joe was on high alert, listening for the slightest movement or sound.

As forward scout, his responsibilities weighed heavily. Five Australian soldiers depended on his skills, trusting that he wouldn't lead them blindly into an ambush.

As he edged around another corner, a sudden crash shattered the silence. Joe's night vision vanished. He was plunged into darkness.

Adrenaline exploded in his vitals. How had he lost his goggles? Or—*hell*—had worse happened? Had he been blinded?

He couldn't even find his damn rifle.

To add to the confusion, a persistent drumming sounded above and around him.

What the hell had happened?

Even more bizarrely, when Joe stepped forward he felt carpet beneath his feet. His *bare* feet. What was going on? Where was he?

Panic flared. Had he gone raving mad? Where were his boots? His weapon?

Totally disoriented, he blinked, and at last his vision cleared slightly. He could just make out the dimmest of details, and he seemed to be naked apart from boxer shorts and, yes, his feet were bare and they were definitely sinking into soft carpet.

He had absolutely no idea where the hell he was, or how he'd got there.

Then he heard a small child's cry and his stomach lurched. As a Commando, in close contact with the enemy, his greatest fear was that he might inadvertently bring harm to Afghan children.

It was still difficult to see as he made his way through the pitch-black night, moving towards the child's cry, bumping into a bookcase.

A bookcase?

A doorway.

Ahead, down a passage, he saw a faint glow—it illuminated painted tongue-and-groove timber walls. Walls that were strangely familiar.

Karinya.

Hell, yeah. Of course.

A soft oath broke from him. He'd woken from a particularly vivid dream and he was back in North Queensland and, while he couldn't explain the crashing sound, the crying child was…

Jacko.

His son.

Joe's heart skidded as he scorched into Jacko's room. In the glow of a night light, he saw the toddler huddled and frightened on the floor in the wreckage of his cot. Without hesitation, Joe dived and swept the boy into his arms.

Jacko was shaking but, in Joe's arms, he nestled against his bare chest, a warm ball sobbing, seeking protection and clearly trusting Joe to provide it.

'Shh.' Joe pressed his lips to the boy's soft hair and caught the amazing smell of shampoo, probably baby shampoo. 'You're OK. I've got you.'

I'm your father.

The boy felt so little and warm in Joe's arms. And so scared. A fierce wave of emotion came sweeping through Joe—a surge of painful yearning—an urge to protect this warm, precious miniature man, to keep him safe at all costs.

'I've got you, little mate,' he murmured. 'You're OK.' And then he added in a soft, tentative whisper, 'I'm your dad. I love you, Jacko.' The words felt both alien and wonderful. And true.

'What happened?' Ellie's voice demanded from the doorway. 'I heard a crash.'

Joe turned and saw her in the dimmed light, wearing a white nightdress with tiny straps, her dark hair tumbling in soft waves about her smooth, bare shoulders. She looked beautiful beyond words and Joe's heart almost stopped.

'What happened?' she asked again, coming forward. 'Is Jacko all right?'

'I think he's fine, but he got a bad fright. Looks like his cot's collapsed.'

Jacko had seen Ellie now and he lurched away from Joe, throwing out his arms and wailing, 'Mummy!'

Joe tried not to mind that his Great Three Seconds of Fatherhood were over in a blink, or that Jacko, now safely in Ellie's arms, looked back at him as if he were a stranger.

Ellie was staring at Joe too—staring with wide, almost popping eyes at his bare chest and at the scars on his shoulder. Joe hoped her gaze wouldn't drop to his shorts or they'd both be embarrassed.

Abruptly, he turned, forcing his attention to the collapsed cot. It was a simple timber construction with panels of railings threaded on a metal rod and screwed into place with wing nuts. Nothing had actually broken. It seemed the thing had simply come apart.

'Looks like the wing nuts in the corners worked loose,' he said.

'Oh, Lord.' Ellie stepped forward with the boy on her hip. 'Jacko was playing with those wing nuts the other day. He was trying to undo them, but I didn't think he had a hope.'

'Well, I'd say he was successful. He must have strong little fingers.'

Ellie looked at her son in disbelief and then she shook her head and gave a wry smile, her dark eyes suddenly sparkling. Joe so wished she wouldn't smile like that, not when she was standing so close to him in an almost see-through nightdress.

'You're a little monkey, Jacko,' she told the boy affectionately. Then, more businesslike, she turned to Joe. 'I guess it shouldn't be too hard to fix?'

'Piece of cake.' He picked up one of the panels. 'A

pair of pliers would be handy. The nuts need to be tight enough to stop him from doing it again.'

Ellie nodded. 'I think I have a spare pair of pliers in the laundry, but don't worry about it now. I'll take Jacko back to my room. He can sleep with me for the rest of the night.'

Lucky Jacko.

From the doorway, she turned and frowned back at Joe. 'Do you need anything? A hot drink or something to help you get back to sleep?'

She must have seen the expression on his face. She quickly dropped her gaze. 'I keep forgetting. You're a tough soldier. You can sleep on a pile of rocks.'

With Jacko in her arms, she hurried away, the white nightdress whispering around her smooth, shapely calves.

Joe knew he wouldn't be sleeping.

Jacko settled quickly. He was like a little teddy bear as he snuggled close to Ellie and in no time he was asleep again. She adored her little miracle boy, and she relished this excuse to lie still and hold him, loving the way he nestled close.

Lying in the darkness, she inhaled the scent of his clean hair and listened to the soft rhythm of his breathing.

His perfection constantly amazed her.

But, tonight, it wasn't long before she was thinking about Joe and, in a matter of moments, she felt a pain in her chest like indigestion, and then her throat was tense and aching, choked.

She kept seeing Joe's signature on that piece of paper.

And now he was about to head off for the Southern

Ocean. Surely, if he wanted adventure, he could have caught wild bulls or rogue crocodiles, or found half a dozen other dangerous activities that were closer to home?

Instead, once again, he was getting as far away from her as possible, risking his life in stormy seas and chasing international poachers, for pity's sake.

Unhelpfully, Ellie recalled how eye-wateringly amazing Joe had looked just now, standing bare-chested in Jacko's room. With the little boy in his arms, he'd looked so incredibly strong and muscular and protective.

Man, he was *buffed*.

He'd always been fit and athletic, of course, which was one of the reasons the Army had snapped him up, but now, after all the extra training and discipline, her ex-husband looked sensational.

Her ex.

The word hit her like a slug to the heart. Which was crazy. *I don't want him back. Looks aren't everything. They're just a distraction.*

Tonight, it was all too easy to forget the pain she and Joe had been through, the constant bickering and soul-destroying negativity, the tears and the yelling. The sad truth was—the final year before their separation had been pretty close to hell on earth.

Unhappily, Ellie knew that a large chunk of the tension had been her fault. During that bleak time when she'd been so overwhelmed by her inability to get pregnant again, she'd really turned on Joe until everything he'd done had annoyed her.

Looking back, she felt so guilty. She'd been a shrew—constantly picking on Joe for the smallest things, even the way he left clothes lying around, or the way he left the lid off the toothpaste, the way he'd assumed she was happy to look after the house and the garden while he swanned off, riding his horse all over their property, enjoying all the adventurous, more important outdoor jobs, while she was left to cook and clean.

Ellie hadn't been proud of her nagging and fault-finding. As a child, she'd hated the way her mother picked on her dad all the time, and she'd been shocked to find herself repeating that despicable pattern. But she'd become so tense and depressed she hadn't been able to stop herself.

Naturally, Joe hadn't accepted her insults meekly. He'd slung back as good as he got. But she'd been devastated when he finally suggested divorce.

'It's clear that I'm making you unhappy,' he'd said in a cold, clipped voice she'd never heard before.

And how could Ellie deny it? She *had* been unhappy, and she'd taken her unhappiness out on Joe, but that hadn't meant she wanted to be rid of him.

'Do you really want a divorce?' she'd asked him and, although she'd been crying on the inside, for the sake of her pride, she'd kept a brave face.

'I think it's the only solution,' Joe had said. 'We can't go on like this. Maybe you'll have better luck with another guy.'

She didn't want another man, but why would Joe believe that when she'd been so obviously miserable?

'What would you do?' she'd asked instead. 'Where would you go? What would we do about Karinya?'

He'd been scarily cool and detached. 'You can make up your mind about Karinya, but I'll apply to join the Army.'

She hadn't known how to fight this. 'The Army was what you wanted all along, wasn't it? It was what you were planning before we met.'

Joe didn't deny this.

It was then she'd known the awful truth. Falling for her had been an aberration. A distraction.

If she hadn't been pregnant, they wouldn't have married…

The bitter memories wrung a groan from Ellie and, beside her in the darkness, Jacko stirred, throwing out an arm and smacking her on the nose. He didn't wake up and she rolled away, staring moodily into the black night, thinking about Joe lying in his swag on the study floor. He'd insisted on sleeping there rather than in Nina's room.

'It's only for one night,' he'd said. 'Not worth disturbing her things.'

Ellie wondered if Joe was asleep, or whether he was also lying there thinking about their past.

Unlikely.

No doubt he was relieved to be finally and permanently free of her. He certainly wouldn't be as mixed-up and tied in knots as she was.

Joe didn't want to think about Ellie. She was part of his past, just as the Army was now. Every time visions of her white nightdress arrived, he forcibly erased them.

He'd signed the final papers.

Ellie. Was. No. Longer. His. Wife.

And yet…

Annoyingly, he felt a weight that felt like grief pressing on his chest. Grief for their loss, and for their failure, for their past mistakes and for how things used to be at the beginning.

And, despite his best efforts, he couldn't stop the blasted memories.

He'd been a goner from the moment he first saw Ellie, which was pretty bizarre, given that his first sighting had been at long distance.

Ellie had been walking with her back to him at the far end of their tiny town's one and only shopping street. And, from the start, there'd been something inescapably alluring about her. The glossy swing of her dark hair and the jaunty sway of her neat butt in long-legged blue jeans had completely captured his attention.

Of course, it was totally the *worst* time for Joe to become romantically entangled. He'd been on the brink of joining the Army. After struggling unsuccessfully to find his place in the large Madden family, overrun with strapping sons, he'd been lured by the military's promise of adventure and danger.

So, on that day that was etched forever in his memory, he should have been able to ignore Ellie's attractions. He should have finished his errands in town and headed back to their cattle property. And perhaps he would have done that if Jerry Bray hadn't chosen that exact moment to step out of the stock and station agency to speak to Ellie.

Jealousy was a strange and fierce emotion, Joe swiftly discovered. He hadn't even met this girl, hadn't yet seen her front-on, hadn't discovered the bewitching sparkle in her eyes. And yet he was furious with Jerry for chatting her up.

To Joe's huge relief, Jerry's boss interrupted his employee's clumsy attempts at flirtation and called him back inside.

Alone once more, Ellie continued on to the Bluebird Café, and this was a golden opportunity Joe couldn't let pass.

After a carefully calculated interval, he followed her into the café, found her sitting alone at one of the tables, drinking a milkshake and engrossed in a women's magazine.

She looked up when he walked in and Joe saw her face for the first time. Saw her eyes, the same lustrous dark brown as her hair, saw her finely arched eyebrows, her soft pale skin, the sweet curve of her mouth, her neat chin. She was even lovelier than he'd imagined.

And then she smiled.

And *zap*. Joe was struck by the proverbial lightning flash. His skin was on fire, his heart was a skyrocket.

'So what d'ya want?' asked Bob Browne, the café's proprietor.

Joe stared at him blankly, unable, for a moment, to think. It was as if his mind had been wiped clean by the dark-eyed girl's smile.

Bob gave a knowing smirk and rolled his eyes. 'She's not on the menu.'

Ignoring this warning, Joe shrugged and ordered a hamburger and a soft drink. Unable to help himself, he crossed the café to the girl's table. 'Hi,' he said.

'Hello.' This time, when she smiled, he saw the most fetching dimple.

'You must be new around here. I don't think we've met. I'm Joe Madden.'

'Ellie Saxby,' she supplied without hesitation.

Ellie Saxby. Ellie. Had there ever been a more delightful name?

'Are you staying around here?' he asked super-casually.

'I'm working for the Ashtons. As a jillaroo.'

Better and better.

There was a spare chair at Ellie Saxby's table. 'OK if I sit here?' Joe was again carefully, casually polite.

Ellie rewarded him with another dazzling smile. 'Sure.'

Her eyes were shining, her cheeks flushed. The atmosphere was so electric, Joe felt as if he was walking on clouds.

And yet there was nothing remarkable about that first conversation. Joe was too dazed to think of anything very clever to say. But he and Ellie chatted easily about where they lived and why they'd come to town.

By the time his hamburger arrived, he was halfway in love with Ellie and she was giving out all the right signals. They left the café together and Joe walked with her to her vehicle.

They exchanged phone numbers and Ellie remained standing beside her car, as if she wasn't ready to drive away.

She looked so alluring, with her sparkling eyes and shiny hair, her soft skin and pretty mouth.

Joe had never been particularly forward with girls, but he found himself saying, 'Look, I know we've just met, and this out of line, but I really need to—'

He didn't even finish the sentence. He simply leaned in and kissed her. Ellie tasted as fresh as spring and, to his amazed relief, she returned his kiss with just the right level of enthusiasm, and a simple hello, exploratory kiss became the most thrilling, most electrifying kiss ever.

It was the start of a whirlwind romance. Before the week was out, he and Ellie had found an excuse to meet again and, within the first month, they drove together to Rockhampton for dinner and a movie, followed by a night in a motel, which proved to be a night of blazing, out of this world passion.

When Ellie discovered she was pregnant, Joe had to make a quick decision. Ellie or the Army?

No contest.

In a blinding flash of clarity, he knew without question that his plan to join the Army had been a crazy idea. In Ellie he'd found his true reason for being. He asked her to marry him and, to his delight, she readily agreed.

The ink on their marriage certificate was barely dry before they headed north in search of their very own cattle property and the start of their bright new happy-ever-after.

When Ellie miscarried three weeks after they'd moved into Karinya, they'd been deeply disappointed but, in the long run, not too downhearted. After all, they were young and healthy and strong and in love.

But it was the start of a downhill run. A diagnosis of endometriosis had followed. Joe had never even heard of this condition, let alone understood how it could blight such a fit and healthy girl. Ellie was vivacious, bursting with energy and life and yet, over the next few years, she was slowly dragged down.

He remembered finding her slumped over the kitchen table, her face streaked with tears.

He'd touched her gently on the shoulder, stroked her

hair. 'Don't let it get you down, Ellie. It'll be OK. We'll be OK.'

We still have each other, he'd wanted to say.

But she'd whirled on him, her face red with fury. 'How can you say that? How can you possibly *know* we'll be OK? I'm sorry, Joe, but that's just a whitewash, and it makes me *so* mad!'

She'd lost all hope, had no faith in him or their future. He'd felt helpless.

Now, with hindsight, he could see the full picture. He and Ellie had rushed at marriage like lemmings to a cliff, expecting to build a lasting relationship— for richer or poorer, in sickness and in health— having based these expectations on little more than blazing lust.

It was his fault.

Joe had always known that. Looking back, it was blindingly obvious that he hadn't courted Ellie properly. They hadn't taken anywhere near enough time to get to know each other as friends before they became life partners. They hadn't even fully explored their hopes and dreams before they'd embarked on marriage.

They'd simply been lovers, possessed by passion, a heady kind of madness. And Ellie had found herself trapped by that first pregnancy.

Small wonder their marriage had hit the rocks as soon as the seas got rough and, instead of offering Ellie comfort, Joe had taken refuge, working long hard hours in Karinya's paddocks—fencing, building dams, mustering and branding cattle. Later he'd joined the Army. Had that been a kind of refuge as well?

Whatever. It was too late for an extensive post-mortem. Tomorrow he'd be leaving again and Ellie would finally be free. He wished he felt better about that.

CHAPTER FOUR

NEXT MORNING IT was raining harder than ever.

Out of habit, Ellie woke early and slipped out of bed, leaving Jacko curled asleep. She dressed quickly and went to the kitchen and, to her surprise Joe was already up, dressed and drinking a mug of tea.

He turned and greeted her with only the faintest trace of a smile. 'Morning.'

'Good morning.' Ellie flicked the kettle to bring it back to the boil and looked out of the window at the wall of thick grey rain. 'It's been raining all night. You won't want to waste time getting over the river.'

Joe nodded. 'I'll need to get going, but I'm worried about you and Jacko. You could be cut off.'

'Yeah, well, that happens most wet seasons.' She reached for a mug and a tea bag. 'I'm used to it and we're well stocked up.'

Joe was frowning, and Ellie wondered if frowning was his new default expression.

'It's hardly an ideal situation,' he said. 'A woman and a little child, isolated and alone out here. It's crazy. What if Jacko gets sick or injured?'

'Crikey, Joe. Since when has that worried you? We've been living here since he was born, you know.'

'But you haven't been cut off by flood waters.'

'I have, actually.'

He glared at her, and an emotion halfway between anger and despair shimmered in his eyes.

Ellie tried for nonchalance as she poured boiling water into her mug.

Joe cleared his throat. 'I think I should stay.'

Startled, Ellie almost scalded herself. 'You mean stay here with us?'

'Just till the river goes down again.'

'Joe, we're divorced.'

His blue eyes glittered. 'I'm aware of that.'

'And…and it's almost Christmas.' Last night they'd struggled through an unbearably strained meal together. They couldn't possibly manage something as festive as Christmas.

Ellie was supposed to be spending Christmas Day with her neighbours and good friends, the Andersons, although, if the creek stayed high, as well as the river, that might not be an option.

Of course, her mother had originally wanted her to go home to New South Wales, but Ellie had declined on several grounds. Number one—she wasn't comfortable around her stepfather, for reasons her mother had turned a deaf ear to. As well as that, up until yesterday, she'd been dealing, ironically, with drought. Her priority had been the state of her cattle—and then clearing things up with Joe.

The Joe factor was well and truly sorted, and sharing Christmas with him would be a disaster. Being divorced and forced to stay together would be a thousand times bigger strain than being married and apart.

'There's absolutely no need for you to stay, Joe. I really don't think it's a good idea.'

'It was just a suggestion,' he said tightly. 'I was only thinking of your safety.'

'Thanks. That's thoughtful.' Feeling awkward, Ellie fiddled with the handle of her tea mug. 'You know drought and floods are part and parcel of living in this country.'

With a brief shrug, Joe drained his mug and placed it in the sink. 'I should head off then, before the river gets any higher.'

'But you haven't had breakfast.'

'As you pointed out, it wouldn't be wise to wait. It's been raining all night and the river's rising every minute. I've packed the solicitor's papers. I'll drop them in at Bligh's office.'

'Right.' Ellie set her tea mug aside, no longer able to drink it.

Joe's duffel bag was already packed and zipped, and the swag he'd used for sleeping on the study floor was neatly rolled and strapped. Seemed the Army had turned him into a neat freak.

'I've also fixed Jacko's cot,' he said.

'You must have got up early.'

Without answering, he reached for his duffel bag and swung it over one shoulder. 'I wasn't sure where to put the Christmas presents, so I stowed them under the desk in the study. Hope that's OK?'

'That…that's fine, thanks, Joe.' Ellie wished she didn't feel quite so downbeat. 'I hope you haven't spoiled Jacko with too many presents.'

She winced as she said this. She didn't really mind how many presents Joe had bought. This was one of his few chances to play the role of a father. She'd been try-ing for a light-hearted comment and had totally missed the mark.

Now, Joe's cold, hollow laugh chilled her to the bone.

His face seemed to be carved from stone as he turned to leave. 'Well, all the best, Ellie.'

'Hang on. I'll wake Jacko so you can say goodbye to him, too.'

'Don't disturb him.'

'You've got to say goodbye.' Ellie was close to tears. 'Actually, we'll come out to the river crossing with you. We can follow you in the ute. Just in case there's a problem.'

'There won't be a problem.'

To her dismay, her tears were threatening to fall. 'Joe, humour me. I want to see you safely off this property.'

For the first time, a faint smile glimmered. 'Of course you do.'

Ellie parked on a ridge above the concrete causeway that crossed the river and peered through the rain at the frothing, muddy flood rushing below.

She could see the bright blue of Joe's hire car parked just above the waterline and his dark-coated figure standing on the bank, hands on hips as he studied the river.

'I think it's already too high,' she said glumly to Jacko. The river level was much, much higher than she'd expected. Clearly, the waters from the north had already reached them overnight.

She felt a flurry of panic. Did this mean that Joe would have to stay with them for Christmas after all? How on earth would they cope with the strain?

Even as she wondered this, Joe took off his coat, tossed it back into his vehicle, then began to walk back to the swirling current.

He wasn't going in there, surely?

'Joe!' Ellie yelled, leaping out of the ute. 'Don't be mad. You can't go in there.'

He showed no sign that he'd heard her. No doubt he was as keen to leave her as she was to see him go, but marching into a racing torrent was madness.

Ellie rushed down the track. 'Joe, stop!' The river was mud-brown and seething. 'You can't go in there,' she panted as she reached him.

He scowled and shook his head. 'It's OK. I just need to check the condition of the crossing and the depth. It's too risky to drive straight in there, but I can at least test it on foot. I'll be careful. I think it's still shallow enough to get the car across.'

'But look how fast the water's running. I know you're keen to get away, but you don't have to play the tough hero now, Joe.' Knowing how stubborn he could be, she tried for a joke. 'I don't want to have to tell Jacko that his father was a moron who was washed away trying to cross a flooded river.'

Joe's blue eyes flashed through the sheeting rain. 'I've been trained to stay alive, not to take senseless risks.' He jerked his head towards the ute. 'If you're worried about Jacko, you should get back up there and stay with him.'

Ellie threw up her hands in despair. She'd more or less encouraged, or rather *urged*, Joe to leave. But as she stood there debating how to stop her ex from risking his neck, she heard her little son calling to her.

'Go to him,' ordered Joe.

Utterly wretched, she began to walk back up the slope, turning every step to look over her shoulder as Joe approached the river. By the time she reached the ute, Joe was already in the water and in no time he was up to his knees.

Anxiously, she watched as he carefully felt the ground in front of him with one foot. He edged forward but, despite the obvious care he was taking, a sudden swift surge in the current buffeted him, making him sidestep to regain his balance.

'Joe!' she yelled, sticking her head out into the rain. 'That's enough! Get out!'

'Joe, that's 'nuff!' parroted Jacko.

A tree branch hurtled past Joe, almost sweeping him with it.

Turn back. Ellie was urging him, under her breath now, so she didn't alarm Jacko.

To her relief, Joe must have realised his venture was useless. At last he turned and began to make his way back to the bank.

But Ellie's relief was short-lived, of course. Sure, she was grateful that Joe hadn't drowned himself, but she had no idea how they could live together amicably till the river levels dropped. It would take days, possibly weeks, and the strain would be intolerable.

She was so busy worrying about the challenge of sharing Christmas with her ex that she didn't actually see what happened next.

It seemed that Joe was standing perfectly upright one moment, and then he suddenly toppled sideways and his dark head disappeared beneath the ugly brown water.

Joe had no warning.

He had a firm footing on the causeway, but with the

next step there was no concrete beneath him and he was struggling to regain his balance. Before he could adjust his weight, he slid off the edge.

He felt a sudden jarring scrape against his leg as he was pulled down into the bowels of the dark, angry river.

He couldn't see, couldn't breathe.

Scorching pain shot up his calf, and now he discovered that he also couldn't move. His foot was jammed between the broken section of the concrete causeway and a rock.

Hell. This was it. He'd survived four years of war and now he was going to die here. In front of Ellie and Jacko.

He was a brainless idiot. What had Ellie called him? A moron. She was dead right. No question.

And now… As his lungs strained for air, frantic memories flashed. The first time he'd seen Ellie in the outback café. The first time they'd kissed.

Last night and the chubby, sweet weight of Jacko in his arms.

His signature, acknowledging their divorce.

Don't freaking panic, man.

This was a major stuff-up, but he'd been trained to think.

He had to forget about the pain in his leg and his dire need for air and he had to work out a plan. Fast.

Clearly, his first priority was to get his head above water, but he was anchored by his trapped leg and the massive force of the rushing river. There was only one possible course of action. He had to brace against the current and use every ounce of his upper body strength, especially his stomach muscles, to pull himself upright.

Almost certainly, he couldn't have done it without

his years in the Army and its daily routine of rugged physical training.

As he fought his way upright, his arm bumped a steel rod sticking out of the concrete. As soon as he grabbed it, he had the leverage to finally lift his head above the surface.

He dragged a great, gasping gulp of air. And immediately he heard Ellie's cry.

'Joe! Oh, God, Joe!'

She was in the river, making her way towards him through the seething, perilous water. Her dark hair was plastered to her head, framing her very white, frightened face, and she looked too slender and too fragile and too totally vulnerable.

At any moment, she would be whipped away downstream and Joe knew he wouldn't have a chance in hell of saving her. In the same moment, he thought of trusting little Jacko strapped in his car seat, needing Ellie.

'Get back,' he roared to her. 'Stay on the bank. I'm OK.'

'You're not. Let me help you.'

'No,' he bellowed angrily. '*Get back!*'

He, at least, had something to hang on to, which was more than Ellie had. 'There's no point in both of us getting into trouble. If you're washed away, I won't be able to help you. For God's sake, Ellie, stay there. Think of Jacko. What happens to him, if neither of us gets out?'

This seemed to get through to her at last. She stood there with the river seething about her ankles, clearly tormented by difficult choices, but at least she'd stopped stubbornly coming towards him.

Joe knew he had to get moving. His foot was still

jammed and his only hope was to ignore the pain and to haul his foot out of the trapped boot.

Clenching his teeth, he kept a death grip on the steel rod as he concentrated every sinew in his body into getting his foot free. The force of the river threatened to push him off balance. Slicing pain sheared up his leg as if it was once again sliced by something rough and hard, but somehow, miraculously, his foot was finally out.

Now he just had to stay upright as he fought his way back. He was limping and he stumbled twice, his bare foot slipping on rocks, but he didn't fall and, as he reached the shallows, Ellie was there beside him.

'Don't argue, Joe. Just give me your arm.'

He was happy to let her help him to the bank.

At last…

'Thanks,' he said. And then, with difficulty, 'I'm sorry.'

'Yeah, well, thank God it's over.' Ellie seemed to be suddenly self-conscious. She quickly let go of him and stepped away. Her hair was sleek and straight from the rain and her clothes were plastered to her slender body. And, now that they were safe, Joe probably looked at her for longer than he should have as they stood on the muddy bank, catching their breath.

'You're bleeding!' Ellie cried suddenly, her eyes widening with horror as she pointed to his injured leg.

Joe looked down. Blood was running from beneath his ripped jeans and spreading in bright red rivulets over his bare foot.

'I think it's just a cut,' he said.

'But we need to attend to it. I hope it won't need stitches.'

'I'm sure it's not urgent. Go to Jacko.'

As if backing up Joe's suggestion, a tiny voice in the

distance screamed, 'Mama!' The poor little kid was wailing.

'He needs you,' Joe said, shuddering at the imagined scenario of poor Jacko abandoned in the car while both his parents were swept away.

At least Ellie was already on her way to him. 'You'd better come too,' she called over her shoulder.

There was only one option. While Ellie comforted Jacko, Joe found a towel to wrap around his bleeding leg and, after that, they drove their respective vehicles back to the homestead.

'Nuisance, I know,' Joe said as he set his luggage on the veranda again. 'This totally stuffs up your plans.'

Ellie shrugged. She'd morphed from the bravely stubborn warrior woman who'd rescued him from the river back to a tight-faced, wary hostess.

'We should take a closer look at your leg,' was all she said.

'I don't want to bleed all over the house.' Joe's leg was stinging like crazy and he'd already left bloody footprints on the veranda.

'Let me take a look at it.' Ellie dropped to her knees beside him, frowning as she carefully parted the torn denim to examine his leg more closely.

This was the first time Ellie had touched him in years, and now she was kneeling at his feet and looking so worried. He felt momentarily deprived of air, as if he was back in the river.

Ellie felt incredibly flustered about patching up Joe's leg.

She'd been hoping for distance from her ex, and here

she was instead, tending to his wounds. And the task felt impossibly, disturbingly intimate. She knew she had to get a grip. It was only a matter of swabbing Joe's leg, for heaven's sake. What was wrong with her?

Of course, she was still shaken from the shock of seeing him almost drown in front of her. She kept reliving that horrifying moment when his dark head had disappeared beneath the swirling flood water.

She'd believed it was the end—Joe was gone for ever—and she'd been swamped by an agonising sense of loss. A slug of the darkest possible despair.

Even now, after they were both safely home and showered and changed, she felt shaky as she gathered bottles of antiseptic, tubes of cream and cotton wool swabs and bandages and anything else she thought she might need.

Now she could see the contrariness of their situation. She and Joe had made every attempt to split, finally and for ever, and yet fate had a strange sense of humour and had deemed it necessary to push them together again.

Here was Joe in her kitchen, dressed in shorts, with his long brown leg propped on a chair.

It wasn't fair, Ellie decided, that despite an angry red gash, a single limb could look so spectacularly masculine, so strongly muscled and large.

'Blood,' little Jacko announced solemnly, stepping closer to inspect the bright wound on Joe's calf.

'Jacko's always seriously impressed by blood,' she explained.

Jacko looked up at Joe with round worried eyes, blue gaze meeting blue. 'Band-Aid,' he pronounced solemnly.

'Thanks, mate.' Joe smiled at the boy. 'Your mum's looking after me, so I know I'm in good hands.'

To Ellie's dismay, she felt a bright blush heat her face. 'I'm afraid Joe will need more than a Band-Aid,' she said tightly as she drew a chair close. 'Jacko, why don't you go and find Teddy? I'll give him a Band-Aid, too.' With luck, she would get most of this task done while the boy was away, looking for his favourite stuffed toy.

But, to her annoyance, she couldn't quite meet Joe's eyes as she bent forward to examine his torn flesh. 'It looks like a very bad graze—and it's right down your shin.' She couldn't help wincing in sympathy. 'It must have hurt.'

'It's not too bad. I don't think it's too deep, do you?'

'Perhaps not, but it's had all that filthy river mud in it. I'd hate you to get infected.' Gently, conscientiously, Ellie washed the wound with warm water and antiseptic, then dabbed at the ragged edges with a cotton wool swab and extra antiseptic. 'I hope this doesn't sting too much.'

'Just slosh it on. I'll be fine.'

Of course. He was a tough guy.

Ellie wished she was tougher. She most definitely wished that being around her ex-husband didn't make her feel so breathless and trembling. And overheated.

She forced herself to be businesslike. 'Are you up-to-date with your tetanus shots?'

'No worries there. The Army made sure of it.'

'Of course. OK. I think I should put sterile dressings on these deeper patches.'

'I'm damn lucky you have such a well stocked first aid kit.'

'The Flying Doctors provided it. There are antibiotics, too, if you need them.'

'You're an angel, Ellie.'

Joe said this with such apparent sincerity she was terrified to look him in the eye, too worried he'd read her emotions, that he'd guess how upset she'd been by his accident, that he'd sense how his proximity set her pulses hammering.

Carefully, she tore the protective packaging from a dressing patch and placed it on his leg, gently pressing the adhesive edges to seal it to his skin. Then, without looking up, she dressed another section, working as swiftly and efficiently, and as gently, as she could.

'The Florence Nightingale touch suits you.'

Ellie's head snapped up and suddenly she was looking straight into Joe's eyes. His bright blue gorgeous eyes that had robbed her of common sense and stolen her heart at their very first meeting.

Joe responded with a slow shimmering smile, as if he liked looking at her, too. Her face flamed brightly. Dismayed, she clambered to her feet.

'Teddy!' hollered Jacko, suddenly running into the room with his fluffy golden bear.

Excessively grateful for the distraction, Ellie found a fluorescent green child-pleasing Band-Aid and ceremoniously applied it to the bear's furry leg. Jacko was suitably delighted and he showed the bear to Joe, who inspected the toy's injury with commendable attention for a man not used to children.

'OK,' Ellie told Joe brusquely as Jacko trotted off again, happily satisfied. 'You can throw your things into Nina's room. You should be comfortable enough sleeping in there.'

This time she was ready when a blush threatened at the mere mention of his sleeping arrangements. A deep breath and the sheer force of willpower kept it at bay, but she didn't miss the flash of tension in Joe's eyes.

Almost immediately, however, Joe recovered, and he gave her an easy shrug. 'I'm fine with sleeping in the swag.'

'Don't be silly. You can't sleep on the study floor with an injured leg.'

His shoulders lifted in a shrug. 'OK. I'm not fussy. I'll sleep wherever's most convenient for you.'

Their gazes locked and Ellie's pulses drummed. She knew Joe must have been thinking, as she was, of the big double bed where she slept. Alone. The bed they'd once shared so passionately.

Hastily she blocked out the dangerously stirring memories of their intimacy, but, as she put the first aid kit away, she wondered again how she was going to survive several days of Joe's presence in her house. She felt quite sure she'd already stumbled at the first hurdle.

CHAPTER FIVE

JOE'S BROTHER, HEATH, answered when Joe rang home with the news that he couldn't make it for Christmas,

'Jeez, mate, that's bad luck.'

'I know. I'm sorry, but with all this rain it's impossible to get through.'

'Mum will be upset.'

'Yeah.' Joe grimaced. It was way too long since he'd been home. 'So, how are Mum and Dad?'

'Both fighting fit.' Heath laughed. 'Excuse the pun. Should remember I'm talking to a soldier.'

'Former soldier.'

'Yeah. Anyway, they were really excited about seeing you.'

Joe suppressed a sigh. 'I suppose Dad's busy?'

'He and Dean are out in the paddock helping a heifer that's having twins. But Mum's around.'

'I'd like to speak to her.'

'Sure. She's just in the kitchen, up to her elbows in her usual Christmas frenzy. Making shortbread today, I think. I'll get her in a sec—but first, tell me, mate—if you're stuck at Karinya, does that mean you'll have to spend Christmas with Ellie?'

'Looks that way.' Joe tried hard to keep his voice neutral.

'But you're still going ahead with the divorce, aren't you?'

'Sure. Everything's signed, but I can't deliver the final paperwork till the rivers go down. As far as we're both concerned, though, it's a done deal. All over, red rover.'

'Hell. And now you're stuck there together. That's tough.'

'Well, at least I get to spend more time with Jacko.'

'That's true, I guess,' Heath said slowly, making no attempt to hide his doubts. 'Just the same, you have my sympathy, Joe.'

'Thanks, but I don't really need it. Ellie and I are OK. We're being perfectly civil.'

'Civil? Sounds like a load of laughs.'

'You were going to get Mum?' Joe reminded his brother.

'Yeah, sure. Well, Happy Christmas.'

'Thanks. Same to you, and give my love to Laura and the girls.'

'Will do. And good luck with you know who!'

Joe didn't have long to ponder his brother's final remark. In no time he heard his mother's voice.

'Darling, how lovely to hear from you. But Heath's just told me the terrible news. I can't believe you're stranded! What a dreadful shame, Joe. Are you sure there's no way you can get across that darned river?'

'I nearly drowned myself trying.' Joe wouldn't normally have shared this detail with his mother, but today it was important she understood there was no point in holding out hope.

'Oh, good heavens,' she said. 'Well, I guess there's no hope of seeing you for Christmas.'

'Impossible, I'm afraid.'

'That's *such* a pity.'

In the awkward silence, Joe tried to think of something reassuring to tell her. He'd felt OK before talking to his family but, now that he'd heard their voices, he felt a tug of unanticipated emotion. And nostalgia. He was remembering the happy Christmases of his past.

'So, how are you?' his mother asked after she'd digested his news.

'I'm fine, thanks. Copped a bit of a scrape on the leg, trying to cross the river, but nothing to worry about.'

'And how's Jacko?' His mother's voice softened, taking on a wistful quality.

His parents had never met Jacko, their grandson, and now the sadness in her voice was a stinging jolt, like a fish hook in Joe's heart. He'd told himself that his parents probably didn't mind—after all, they had six other grandkids—but there was no denying the regret in his mother's voice.

'Jacko's a great little bloke,' he told her. 'I'll email photos.'

'That would be lovely. I'm sure he's a dear little boy, just like you were.'

It was hard to know how to respond to this, especially as his throat had tightened painfully. 'He's a cute kid, all right. Gets up to mischief.'

'Oh, the little sweetheart. I can just imagine. Joe, we'll still get to meet Jacko, won't we? Even though you're divorced?'

'Yes. I'll make sure of it.' *Somehow. Some time*. Joe added silently. He wasn't sure when. But it hit him now that it was important for Jacko to meet his side of the family.

He imagined the boy meeting the raft of Madden uncles and cousins—meeting Joe's parents. It hadn't occurred to him till now, but he wanted the boy to know the whole picture. It was important in shaping his sense of identity.

Hell. He'd been so busy carving out a new life for himself that he hadn't given his responsibilities as a father nearly enough thought.

Now, he thought about Christmas at Ridgelands. He could picture it clearly, with the long table on the homestead veranda groaning beneath the weight of food. There'd be balloons and bright Christmas decorations hanging from posts and railings. All his family around the table. His parents, his brothers and their wives and their kids...

They would have a cold seafood salad as a starter, followed by roast turkey and roast beef, all the vegetables and trimmings. Then his mother's Christmas pudding, filled with the silver sixpences she'd saved from decades ago. Any lucky grandchild who scored a sixpence in their pudding could exchange it for a dollar.

There would be bonbons and silly hats and streamers. Corny jokes, family news and tall stories.

When Joe had first arrived back from Afghanistan, he'd been too distanced from his old life to feel homesick. Now, he was seized by an unexpected longing.

'Oh, well,' his mother was saying, 'for the time being, you'll have to give Jacko an extra hug from me.'

'Will do.' Joe swallowed. 'And I'll make sure I come to see you before I leave for the new job.'

'Oh, yes, Joe. Please do come. It's been so long. Too long.'

'I know. I'll be there. I promise. Give my love to Dad, and everyone.'

'Yes, darling. We'll speak again. Can we call you on this number?'

'Sure.'

'And you give my love to—' His mother paused and ever so slightly sighed. 'Perhaps I should say—give my *regards* to Ellie.'

'You can send Ellie your love.' Joe's throat was extra-sore now, as if he'd swallowed gravel. 'She's always liked *you*, Mum. *I'm* her problem.'

'Oh, darling,' An unhappy silence lapsed. 'I just hope you and Ellie manage to have a stress-free Christmas together.'

'We'll be fine. Don't worry. We're on our best behaviour.'

Joe felt a little shaken as he hung up. While he'd been a soldier on active duty, his focus had been on a foreign enemy. With the added problem of an impending divorce hanging over him, he'd found it all too easy to detach himself from home.

Now, for the first time, he began to suspect that avoiding his family had been a mistake. And yet, here he was, about to run away again.

He'd barely put down the receiver when the phone rang almost immediately. He supposed it was his mother ringing back with one last 'thought'.

He answered quickly. 'Hello?'

'Is that Joe?' It was a completely different woman's voice.

'Yes, Joe speaking.'

'Oh.' The caller managed to sound disappointed and put out, as if she was wrinkling her nose at a very unpleasant smell. 'I was hoping to speak to Ellie.'

'Is that you, Angela?' Joe recognised the icy tones of his ex mother-in-law.

'Yes, of course.'

'Ellie's out in the shed, hunting for Christmas decorations. I'll get her to call you as soon as she gets in.'

'So where's Jacko?' Angela Fowler's voice indicated all too clearly that she didn't trust Joe to be alone with her grandson.

'He's taking a nap.'

'I see,' Angela said doubtfully and then she let out a heavy sigh. 'I rang, actually, because I heard about all the rain up there in Queensland on the news. There was talk of rivers flooding.'

'Yes, that's right, I'm afraid. Our local creeks and rivers are up and Karinya's already cut off.'

'Oh, Joe! And you're still there? Oh, how dreadful for poor Ellie.' Ellie's mother had always managed to imply that any unfortunate event in their marriage was entirely Joe's fault. 'Don't tell me this means… It doesn't mean you'll be up there with Ellie and Jacko for Christmas, does it?'

'I'm afraid we don't have a choice, Angela.'

There was a horrified gasp on the end of the line and then a longish bristling pause.

'I'll tell Ellie you called,' Joe said with excessive politeness.

'I suppose, if she's busy, that will have to do.' Reluctantly, Angela added, 'Thanks, I guess.' And then… 'Joe?'

'Yes?'

'I hope you'll be sensitive.'

Joe scowled and refused to respond.

'You've made life hard enough for my daughter.'

His grip on the phone receiver tightened and he was tempted to hurl the bloody phone through the kitchen window. Somehow he reined in his temper.

'You can rest easy, Ange. Ellie has served me with the divorce papers and I've signed on the dotted line. I'll be out of your daughter's hair just as soon as these rivers go down. In the meantime, I'll be on my best behaviour. And I hope you and Harold have a very happy Christmas.'

He was about to hang up when he heard Ellie's footsteps in the hall.

'Hang on. You're in luck. Here's Ellie now.'

Setting down the phone with immense relief, he went down the hallway. Ellie was on the veranda. She'd taken off her rain jacket and was hanging it on the wall hook, and beside her were two large rain-streaked cardboard cartons.

'Your mother's on the phone,' Joe told her.

A frown drew her finely arched eyebrows together. 'OK, thanks.' She was still frowning as she set off down the hall. 'I think Jacko's awake,' she called back to Joe. 'Can you check?'

'Can do.'

Even before Joe reached the boy's room, he heard soft, happy little chuckles. The lively baby talk was such a bright, cheerful contrast to his recent phone conversation.

In fact, Joe couldn't remember ever hearing a baby's laughter before. It was truly an incredible sound.

He slowed his pace as he approached the room and

opened the door slowly, carefully, and he found Jacko, with tousled golden hair and sleep-flushed cheeks, standing in his cot. The little boy was walking his teddy bear, complete with its fluoro Band-Aid, along the railing. He was talking to the bear in indecipherable gibberish. Giggling.

So cute.

So damn cute.

Joe felt a slam, like a fist to his innards. The last time he'd seen his son, he'd been a helpless baby, and now he was a proper little person—walking and talking and learning to play, beginning to imagine.

He'd missed so many milestones.

What will he be like next time I see him?

It was difficult enough that Joe had to spend this extra time with Ellie, while trying to ignore the old tug of an attraction that had never really died. But now, here was his son jerking his heart-strings as well.

As soon as Jacko saw Joe, he dropped the teddy bear and held up round little arms. 'Up!' he demanded.

Joe crossed to the cot and his son looked up at him with a huge, happy grin. It might even have been an admiring grin. A loving grin?

Whatever it was, it hefted a raw punch.

'Up, Joe!'

'OK, mate. Up you come.'

Jacko squealed with delight as Joe swung him high, over the side of the cot. Then, for a heady moment, Joe held the boy in his arms, marvelling at his softness, at his pink and gold perfection.

Hell. He could remember when this healthy, bouncing kid had been nothing more than a cluster of frozen invisible cells in a laboratory—one of the *sproglets* that had caused him and Ellie so much hope and heartbreak.

Now the collection of cells was Jacko, their miraculous solo survivor.

And, after everything they'd been through, Joe found himself in awe.

'Wee-wee!' announced Jacko, wriggling with a need to be out of Joe's arms.

He quickly set the kid down. 'Do you want the toilet?'

Jacko nodded and clutched at the front of his shorts, pulling a face that made the matter look urgent.

'Let's go.' With a hand on his shoulder, Joe guided him quickly down the hallway to the bathroom, realising as he did so that, despite having several young nieces and nephews, *this* was a brand new experience.

'I think you have to stand on this fellow,' he said, grabbing a plastic turtle with a flat, step-like back and positioning it in front of the toilet bowl.

Jacko was red-faced as he climbed onto the step and tugged helplessly at the elastic waistband on his shorts. It was a moment before Joe realised he was needed to help the boy free of his clothing, which included pulling down a miniature pair of underpants printed with cartoon animals.

'OK. There you go. You're all set now.'

And then, out of nowhere, a fleeting memory from his own childhood flashed. Tearing a corner of paper from the roll on the wall, Joe dropped it into the bowl.

'See if you can pee on the paper,' he said.

Jacko looked up at him with open-mouthed surprise, but then he turned back and, with commendable concentration, did exactly as Joe suggested.

The kid was smart.

And right on target.

'Bingo!' Joe grinned. 'You did it. Good for you, Jacko!'

Jacko beamed up at him. 'Bingo, Joe!'

'You've earned a high five!' Joe held out his hand.

'What are you two up to?'

They both turned to find Ellie in the hallway behind them, hands on hips. Beautiful but frowning.

'I did Bingo, Mummy,' Jacko announced with obvious pride as he stood on the turtle with his shorts around his ankles.

'Bingo? What are you talking about?' She directed her frown at Joe.

He pointed into the bowl. 'Jacko hit the piece of paper. I thought it would help him to aim.'

'Aim?' Ellie stared at him, stared at both of them, her dark eyes frowning with disbelief. As comprehension dawned, her mouth twisted into the faintest glimmer of a smile—a smile that didn't quite make it.

'He's not in the Army *yet*,' she said tightly. 'And don't forget to wash your hands, Jacko. It's time for your afternoon tea.'

'So, do you have a job for me?' Joe asked once Jacko was perched on a stool at the kitchen bench and tucking into a cup of juice and a plate of diced cheese and fruit.

Ellie looked pained—an expression Joe was used to seeing after a phone call from her mother. No doubt Angela Fowler had once again piled on the sympathy for her poor daughter's terrible fate—this time, being forced to spend Christmas with her dropkick ex.

In the past, that pained look had irritated Joe. Today, he was determined to let it wash over him.

'Perhaps I could assemble the Christmas tree?' he suggested.

'That would be helpful.' Ellie didn't follow through with a smile. 'The tree's in one of the boxes on the veranda.'

'You'd like it in the lounge room?'

'Yes, please.'

Ellie took a deep breath as she watched Joe head off to the veranda.

Conversations with her mother had always been heavily laced with anti-Joe sentiments and today had been a doozy.

This is a dangerous time for you, Ellie. I don't like the idea of the two of you alone up there. You'll have to be very careful, especially if Joe tries anything.

Tries what, Mum?

Tries to...to win you back.

Of course, Ellie had assured her mother there was no chance of that. Absolutely. No. Chance. But she wished this certainty hadn't left her feeling quite so desolate.

These next few days were going to be hard enough with the two of them stuck in the house while the rain continued pelting down outside. It would be so much easier if she could carry on with the outside work, but the cattle were safe and until the rain stopped there wasn't a lot more she could do.

Unfortunately, she couldn't even give Joe a decent book to read. Since Jacko's birth, she'd only had time for cattle-breeding journals, women's magazines and children's picture books.

Ellie decided to let Joe get on with the tree while she cooled her heels in the kitchen with Jacko, for once letting him dawdle over his food, but as soon as he'd finally downed his afternoon tea, he was keen to be off.

'Where's Joe?' was the first thing he asked.

So they went back to the lounge room and, to Ellie's surprise, Joe had almost finished assembling the six-foot tree. He made it look dead easy, of course.

Jacko stared up at the tree, looking puzzled, as if he couldn't understand why adults would set up a tree inside the house. As an outback boy, he hadn't seen any of the city shops with brightly lit trees and Santa Clauses, although he had vague ideas about Christmas from books and TV.

'This is our *Christmas* tree,' Ellie explained to him. 'Mummy's going to make it pretty with lights and decorations, and soon there'll be lots of presents underneath it.'

At the mention of presents Jacko clapped his hands and took off, running in circles.

'Well, that got a reaction,' said Joe, amused.

'He can still remember the pile of presents he scored for his second birthday.'

Too late, Ellie remembered that Joe hadn't sent the boy anything. Lordy, today there seemed to be pitfalls in even the simplest conversation.

Joe was grim-faced as he fitted the final top branches in place.

Ellie went to the CD player and made a selection—a jaunty version of *Jingle Bells*. She hoped it would lift the dark mood that had lingered since her mum's annoying dire warnings on the phone.

Determined to shake off the grouchiness, she went

to the second carton and took out boxes of exquisite tree ornaments. Decorating the tree had always been her favourite Christmas tradition. Today it was sure to lift her spirits.

'Ooh! Pretty!' Jacko squealed, coming close to inspect.

'Yes, these ornaments are very pretty, but they're made of glass, Jacko, so you mustn't touch. They can break. I'm going to put them on the tree, and they'll be safe there. They'll make the tree beautiful.'

Jacko watched, entranced, as Ellie hooked bright, delicate balls onto the branches. She knew it was too much to expect him not to touch but, before she could warn him to be *very* gentle, he batted with his hand at a bright red and silver ball.

Ellie dived to stop him and Joe dived too, but they were both too late. The ball fell to the floor and smashed.

Ellie cried out—an instinctive response, but probably a mistake. Immediately, Jacko began to wail.

It was Joe who swept the boy into his arms and began to soothe him.

Ellie was left watching them, feeling strangely left out. She waited for Jacko to turn to her, to reach out his arms for her as he always did when he was upset. But he remained clinging to Joe.

Joe. Her son's new, big strong hero.

She refused to feel jealous. If she was honest, she could totally understand the appeal of those muscular, manly arms.

Once upon a time Joe was my hero, too. My tower of strength.

Now, she would never feel his arms around her again.

Yikes, where had that thought sprung from? *What's the matter with me?*

She hurried out of the room to get a dustpan and broom and, by the time she returned, Jacko had stopped crying.

Joe set him down and the boy stood, sniffling, as he watched Ellie sweep up the glittering broken pieces.

'I told you to be careful,' she felt compelled to remind him as she worked. 'You mustn't touch these pretty ornaments, or they'll break.'

'He's too little to understand,' said Joe.

Ellie glared up at him. 'No, he's not.' *What would Joe know about little kids?*

Joe shrugged and looked around the room. 'Perhaps we can find something more suitable for him to play with. Something like paper chains? They might distract him.'

Ellie had actually been thinking along the same lines and it annoyed her that Joe had made the suggestion first. 'So you're suddenly an expert on raising children?'

'Ellie, don't be like that.'

'Like what?'

Joe simply stared at her, his blue eyes coolly assessing.

Oh, help. It was happening already. All the old tensions were sparking between them—electricity of the worst kind. Dangerous. Lethal.

All she'd wanted was a simple, relaxing afternoon decorating the tree.

'There are paper chains in those shopping bags,' she said, pointing to one of the cartons. Then, summoning her dignity, she rose and took the dustpan back to the kitchen.

By the time she returned, Jacko and Joe had trailed bright paper chains along the shelves of the bookcase and they were now looping them around a tall lamp stand.

The CD was still playing. The singer had moved on to *Deck the Halls*, and Ellie set about decorating the tree again, hoping for peace on Earth and goodwill towards one particular man.

She couldn't deny that Joe was great at playing with their son. Every time Jacko became too curious about the tree, Joe would deflect him. They played hide and seek behind the sofa, and Joe taught Jacko how to crawl on his belly, Commando style. Watching this, Ellie winced, sure that Joe's injured leg must have hurt.

She almost said something about his leg, but held her tongue. He was a big, tough soldier, after all.

Joe hid Jacko's teddy bear behind a cushion and the boy squealed with delight every time he rediscovered the toy. After that, Jacko played the game again and again, over and over.

Ellie tried really hard not to feel left out of their games. She knew that the nanny, Nina, played games like this all the time with Jacko, while she was out attending to chores around the property. But she'd never imagined macho Joe being quite so good with the boy.

It shouldn't have bothered her. It *didn't* bother her. If Joe was proving to be an entertaining father, she was pleased. She was even grateful.

She was. Truly.

Meanwhile, the Christmas tree became a thing of beauty, with delicate ornaments and shiny stars, and trailing lines of lights and silver pine cones.

After Jacko's umpteenth game of hiding the toy bear

behind the cushion, Joe strolled over to inspect Ellie's progress.

'It's looking great,' he said. 'Really beautiful.'

His smile was genuine. Gorgeous? It sent unwanted warmth rippling through her. 'At least it helps to make the house look more festive.'

Joe nodded and touched a pretty pink and purple glass spiral with his fingertips. 'I remember these. We bought them for our very first Christmas.'

To Ellie's dismay, her eyes pricked with the threat of tears. Joe shouldn't be remembering those long ago times when they were still happy and hopeful and so blissfully in love.

'I'd rather not rehash old memories, Joe. I don't think it's helpful.'

She saw a flash of emotion in his eyes. Pain? Her comment hadn't hurt him, surely? Not Joe. He had no regrets. Not about them. He'd gone off to war without a backward glance.

And yet he definitely looked upset.

Ellie wondered if she should elaborate. Try to explain her caution.

But what could she explain? That she hadn't meant to hurt him? That, deep down, she still cared about him? That the memories were painful *because* she cared?

How could those sorts of revelations help them now? They couldn't go back.

Confused, Ellie felt more uptight than ever. She spun away from Joe and began to gather up the empty boxes and tissue paper that had housed the decorations, working with jerky, angry movements.

To her annoyance, Joe simply stayed where he was by the tree, watching her with a thoughtful, searching gaze.

'You could always help to clean up this mess,' she said tightly.

'Yes, ma'am.' He moved without haste, picking up the shopping bags that had housed the paper chains. Crossing the room, he dropped them into one of the cartons and, when he looked at her again, his eyes were as hard and cool as ice. 'You can't let up, can you, Ellie?'

'What do you mean?'

'You're determined to make this hard for both of us.'

'I'm not *trying* to make it hard,' she snapped defensively. 'It *is* hard.'

'Yeah? Well, you're not the only one finding it hard. And it doesn't help when you make it so damn obvious that you can't stand the sight of me.'

Ellie smarted. 'How can you say that?'

'How?' Joe looked at her strangely, as if he thought she'd lost her marbles. 'Because it's the truth. It's why I left four years ago.'

No! The protest burst on her lips, but she was aware that Jacko had stopped playing. He was standing very still, clutching his teddy bear, watching them, his little eyes round with worry.

They were fighting in front of him, which was terrible—the very last thing she wanted.

'If we're going to survive this Christmas,' Joe said tightly, 'you're going to have to try harder.'

Ellie felt her teeth clench. 'I know how to behave. I don't need a lecture.'

'Well, you certainly need something. You need to calm down. And you need to think about Jacko.'

'Are you serious?'

'This atmosphere can't be good for him.'

How dare you? Of course she was thinking about Jacko.

Ellie was stung to the core. Who did Joe think he was, telling her off about her parenting? Was he suggesting she was insensitive to Jacko's needs? Joe, who hardly knew the boy?

She was Jacko's *mother.* She knew *everything* about her son—his favourite food, his favourite toy and favourite picture books. She knew Jacko's fears, the times he liked to sleep, the way he liked to be cuddled.

She'd been through his pregnancy on her own, and she'd given birth to him alone. She'd raised Jacko from day one, nursing him through colic and croup and teething. Later, chickenpox. Jacko's first smile had been for Ellie alone. She'd watched him learn to roll over, to sit up and to crawl, to stand, to walk.

Around the clock, she'd cared for him, admittedly with Nina's help, but primarily on her own.

She and Jacko were incredibly close. Their bond was special. Incredibly special.

How dare Joe arrive here out of the blue and start questioning her mothering skills?

Without warning, her eyes filled with tears. Tears of hurt and anger. Scared she might start yelling and say things she'd regret, she turned and fled from the room.

Damn. What a stuff-up.

As Ellie hurried away, Jacko stared up at Joe with big, sad blue eyes. 'Mummy crying.'

Joe swallowed the boulder that jammed his throat. Why the hell had he started a verbal attack on Ellie? This was *so* not the way he'd wanted to behave.

How do I tell my two-year-old son that I'm the reason his mother's crying?

Anxiety and regret warred in Joe's gut as he crossed the room to the boy and squatted so they were at eye level. 'Listen, little mate. I'm going to go and talk to your mum. To…ah…cheer her up.'

Joe had to try at least. It took two to fight. Two to make peace. He had to pull in his horns, had to make an effort to see this situation from Ellie's point of view.

'I need you to be a good boy and stay here with Ted.' Joe dredged up a grin as he tickled Jacko's tummy.

Obligingly, Jacko giggled.

The kid was so cute. Already Joe knew it was going to be hard to say goodbye.

'How about we hide your bear behind the curtain over there?' he suggested, pointing to the floor-length curtains hanging either end of the deep sash windows that opened onto the veranda. He showed Jacko how to hide the bear behind them, just as they had with the cushions, and the little boy was thrilled.

'Ted!' he squealed, astonished by the big discovery when they lifted the curtain. 'Do it again, Joe!' At least he was all smiles again.

'You have a go at hiding him,' said Joe.

Jacko tried, frowning carefully as he placed the bear behind the curtain. Once again, he lifted the fabric and saw the bear, and he was as excited as a scientist discovering the Higgs boson particle.

'OK, you can play with him here,' Joe said. 'And I'll be back in a tick.'

'OK.'

Reassured that Jacko would be happy for a few minutes at least, Joe went in search of Ellie.

CHAPTER SIX

ELLIE STOOD AT one end of the long front veranda, elbows resting on the railings, staring out at the waterlogged paddocks. The rain had actually stopped for now, but the sky was still heavy with thick, grey clouds, so no doubt the downpour would start again soon.

She wasn't crying. She'd dried her tears almost as soon as she left the lounge room and she was determined that no more would fall. She was angry, not sad. Angry with herself, with her stupid behaviour.

She'd been determined to handle Joe's return calmly and maturely, and when he'd been forced to stay here she'd promised herself she would face that with dignity as well. Instead she'd been as tense and sharp-tongued as a cornered taipan.

She was so disappointed with herself, so annoyed. Why couldn't her behaviour ever live up to her good intentions?

You make it so damn obvious that you can't stand the sight of me.

Did Joe really think that? How could he?

It seemed impossible to Ellie. The sad truth was— the sight of Joe stirred her in ways she didn't want to be stirred. She found herself thinking too often about the way they used to make love.

Really, despite their troubles, there'd been so many happy times, some of them incredibly spontaneous and exciting.

Even now, *irrationally*, she found herself remembering one of the happiest nights of her life—a night that had originally started out very badly.

It had happened one Easter. She and Joe were driving down the highway on their way to visit her mum, but they'd been so busy before they left that they hadn't booked ahead, and all the motels down the highway were full.

'Perhaps we should just keep driving,' Joe had said grimly when they reached yet another town with no spare rooms.

'Driving all night?' she'd asked. 'Isn't that dangerous, Joe? We're both pretty tired.'

He'd reluctantly agreed. 'We'll have to find a picnic ground then and sleep in the car.'

It wasn't a cheering prospect, but Ellie knew they didn't have much choice. While Joe went off to find hamburgers for their dinner, she tried to set the car up as best she could, hoping they'd be comfortable.

She'd shifted their luggage and adjusted their seats to lie back and she'd just finished making pillows out of bundles of their clothing when Joe returned. He was empty-handed and Ellie, who'd been ravenous, felt her spirits sink even lower.

'Don't tell me this town's also sold out of hamburgers?'

'I don't know,' he said simply.

Her stomach rumbled hungrily. 'Are all the shops closed?'

'Don't know that either. It doesn't matter.' Joe's sudden cheeky smile was unforgettably gorgeous. He held up a fancy gold ring, dangling keys. 'I've booked us into the honeymoon suite in the best hotel in town.'

Ellie gasped. 'You're joking.'

Still smiling broadly, Joe shook his head. 'Ridgy-didge.'

'Can…can we afford a honeymoon suite?'

He shrugged, then slipped his arm around her shoulders, pressed a warm kiss to her ear. 'We deserve a bit of comfort. We never had a proper honeymoon.'

It was the best of nights. Amazing, and so worth the extravagance.

All thoughts of tiredness vanished when they walked into their suite and saw the champagne in an ice bucket, a huge vase of long-stemmed white roses and chocolate hearts wrapped in gold foil on their pillows.

Like excited kids, they bounced on the enormous king-sized bed and then jumped into the spa bath until their room service dinner arrived. And they felt like film stars as they ate gourmet cuisine dressed in luxurious white fluffy bathrobes.

And, just for one night, they'd put their worries aside and they'd made love like honeymooners.

I shouldn't be thinking about that now…

Ellie was devastated to realise that she was still as physically attracted to her ex as she'd been on that night. The realisation made her panic.

What a mess.

With a despairing sigh, she sagged against a veranda post. How had she and Joe sunk to this? She'd thought about their problems so many times, but she'd never pin-pointed a particular event that had killed their marriage. It had been much the same as today. Ongoing bicker-ing and building resentments had worn them down and eroded their love.

Death by a thousand cuts.

But why? How? How could she be so tense and angry with a man she still fancied? It wasn't as if she actively disliked Joe.

She supposed they should have seen a marriage guid-ance counsellor years ago.

Joe had been too proud, of course, and Ellie had been too scared—scared that she'd be psychoanalysed and found lacking in some vital way. But if she'd been braver, would it have helped?

She probably would have had to tell the counsellor about her father's death and how unhappy she'd been after that. Worse, she would have had to talk about her stepfather and how she'd run away from him.

Ellie didn't actually believe there was a connection between Harold Fowler and her marriage breakdown, but heaven knew what a counsellor might have made of it. Even now, she still shuddered when she thought about Harold.

And here was the thing: it was the sight of *Harold* that Ellie couldn't stand. Not Joe.

Never Joe.

Her mum had married Harold Fowler eighteen months after her father died, after they'd sold the farm and moved into town. Harold owned the town's main hardware store—he was loud and showy and popu-lar, a big fish in a small country pond. And a couple of years later he was elected mayor. Ellie's mum was thrilled. She loved being the mayor's wife and feeling like a celebrity.

Harold, however, had given Ellie the creeps. Right from the start, just the way he looked at her had made her squirm and feel uncomfortable, and that was before he touched her.

She'd been fifteen when he first patted her on the bum. Over the following months, it had happened a few more times, which was bad enough, but then he came into the bathroom one night when she was in the shower.

He was full of apologies, of course, and he backed out quickly, claiming that he'd knocked and no one had answered. But Ellie had seen the horrible glint in his eyes and she was quite sure he hadn't knocked. Her mother hadn't been home that night, which had made the event extra-scary.

And Harold certainly hadn't knocked the second time he barged in. Again, it had happened on a night when Ellie's mum was away at her bridge club. Ellie was seventeen, and she'd just stepped out of the bath and was reaching for her towel when, without warning, Harold had simply opened her bathroom door.

'Oh, my darling girl,' he said with the most ghastly slimy smile.

Whipping the towel about her, Ellie managed to get rid of him with a few scathing, shrilly screamed words, but she'd been sickened, horrified.

Desperate.

And the worst of it was she couldn't get her mother to understand.

'Harold's lived alone for years,' her mum had said, excusing him. 'He's not used to sharing a house with others. And he hasn't done or said anything improper,

Ellie. You're just at that age where you're sensitive about your body. It's easy to misread these things.'

Her mother had believed what she wanted to, what she needed to.

Ellie, however, had left home for good as soon as she finished school, despite her mother's protests and tears, giving up all thought of university. University students had long, long holidays and she would have been expected to spend too much of that time at home.

She had realised it was futile to press her mother about Harold's creepiness—mainly because she knew how desperate her mother was to believe he was perfect. Harold was such a hotshot in their regional town. He was the mayor, for heaven's sake, and Ellie was afraid that, if she pushed her case, she might cause the whole thing to blow up somehow and become a horrible public scandal.

So she'd headed north to Queensland, where she'd scored a job as a jillaroo on a cattle property. Over the next few years, she'd worked on several properties—a mustering season here, a calving season there. Gradually she'd acquired more and more skills.

On one property she'd joined a droving team and she'd helped to move a big mob of cattle hundreds of kilometres. She was given her own horses to ride every day. And, finally, she was living the country life she'd dreamed of, the life she'd anticipated when she was almost thirteen. Before her father died.

Whenever she phoned home or returned home for the shortest possible visits, she was barely civil to Harold. He got the message. Fortunately, he'd never stepped out of line again, but Ellie would never trust him again either.

Trust…

Thinking about all of this now, Ellie was struck by a thought so suffocating she could scarcely breathe.

Oh, my God. Is that my problem? Trust issues?

That was it, wasn't it?

She clung to the railing, struggling for air. Her problems with Joe had nothing to do with whether or not she was attracted to him. The day they met remained the stand-alone most significant moment of her life.

She'd taken one look at Joe Madden, with his sexy blue eyes, his ruggedly cute looks, his wide-shouldered lean perfection and nicest possible smile, and she'd fallen like a stone.

But I couldn't trust Joe.

When it came to coping with the ups and downs of a long-term marriage, she hadn't been strong enough to deal with her disappointments. She'd lost faith in herself, lost faith in the power of love.

Ellie thought again about her father climbing a windmill and dying before he could keep his promise to her. She thought about her creepy stepfather, who'd broken her trust in a completely different way. By the time she'd married Joe…

I never really expected to be happy. Not for ever. I couldn't trust our marriage to work. It was almost as if I expected something to go wrong.

It was such a shock to realise this now.

Too late.

Way too late.

She'd never even told Joe about her stepfather. She'd left it as a creepy, shuddery, embarrassing part of her past that she'd worked hard to bury.

But that hadn't affected how she'd truly felt about him.

She'd loved Joe.

Despite the mixed-up and messy emotional tornado that had accompanied her fertility issues and ultimately destroyed their marriage, she'd *truly* loved him—even when he'd proposed their divorce and he'd told her he was leaving for the Army.

And now?

Now, she was terribly afraid that she'd never really stopped loving him. But how crazy was that when their divorce was a fait accompli?

No wonder she was tense.

Ellie thumped the railing with a frustrated fist. At the same moment, from down the veranda she heard the squeaky hinge of the French windows that led from the lounge room. Then footsteps. She stiffened, turned to see Joe. He was alone.

She drew a deep breath and braced herself. *Don't screw this up again. Behave.*

'Are you OK?' Joe asked quietly.

'Yes, thanks.'

He came closer and stood beside her at the railing, looking out at the soggy paddocks. 'I'm sorry, Ellie. I'm sorry for getting stuck into you. My timing's been lousy, coming back here at Christmas.'

She shook her head. 'I'm making too big a deal about the whole Christmas thing.'

'But that's fair enough. It's the first Christmas Jacko's been old enough to understand.'

She sighed, felt emotionally drained. Exhausted. 'Where's Jacko now?'

'In the lounge room. Still hiding the bear, I hope. Persistent little guy, isn't he?' Joe slid her a tentative sideways smile.

She sent a shy smile back.

Oh, if only they could continue to smile—or, at the very least, to be civilised. Joe was right. For Jacko's sake, they had to try. For the next couple of days—actually, for the next couple of *decades* till Jacko was an adult, they had to keep up a semblance of friendship.

Friendship, when once they'd been lovers, husband and wife.

'I got my knickers in a twist when you suggested I wasn't sensitive about Jacko,' Ellie admitted. 'It felt unfair. He's always been my first concern.'

'You've done an amazing job with the boy. He's a great little guy. A credit to you.'

The praise surprised her. Warmed her.

'I don't know how you've done it out here on your own,' Joe added.

'The nanny's been great. But I'll admit it hasn't always been easy.' She stole another quick glance at him, saw his deep brow, his wide cheekbones, his slightly crooked nose and strong shadowed jaw. She felt her breathing catch. 'I guess this can't be easy for you now. Coming back from the war and everything.'

When he didn't answer, she tried again, 'Was it bad over there?'

A telltale muscle jerked. 'Sometimes.'

Ellie knew he'd lost soldier mates, knew he must have seen things that haunted him. But Special Forces guys hardly ever talked about where they'd been or what they'd done—certainly not with ex-wives.

'I was one of the lucky ones,' he said. 'I got out of it unscathed.'

Unscathed emotionally? Ellie knew that the Army had changed its tactics, sending soldiers like Joe on shorter but more frequent tours of duty in an effort to minimise post-traumatic stress, but she was quite sure that no soldier returned from any war without some kind of damage.

I haven't helped. This hasn't been a very good home-coming for him.

Quickly, bravely, she said, 'For the record, Joe, it isn't true.'

He turned, looking at her intently. 'What do you mean?' His blue eyes seemed to penetrate all the way to her soul.

Her heart began to gallop. She couldn't back down now that she'd begun. 'What you said before—that I can't bear the sight of you—it's not true.' *So not true.*

'That's the way it comes across.'

'I know. I'm sorry. Really sorry.'

She could feel the sudden stillness in him, almost as if she'd shot him. He was staring at her, his eyes burning. With doubt?

Ellie's eyes were stinging. She didn't want to cry, but she could no longer see the paddocks. Her heart was racing.

She almost told Joe that she actually *fancied* the sight of him. Very much. Too much. *That* was her problem. That was why she was tense.

But it was too late for personal confessions. Way too late. Years and years too late.

Instead she said, 'I know I've been stupidly tense about *everything*, but it's certainly not because I can't stand the sight of you.' *Quite the opposite.*

She blinked hard, wishing her tears could air-dry.

Joe's knuckles were white as he gripped the veranda railing and she wondered what he was thinking. Feeling. Was he going over her words?

It's certainly not because I can't stand the sight of you.

Could he read between the lines? Could he guess she was still attracted? Was he angry?

It felt like an age before he spoke.

Eventually, he let go of the railing. Stepped away and drew a deep breath, unconsciously drawing her attention to his height and the breadth of his shoulders. Then he rested his hands lightly on his hips, as if he was deliberately relaxing.

'OK, here's a suggestion,' he said quietly. 'It's Christmas Eve tomorrow. Why don't we declare a truce?'

'A truce? For Christmas?'

'Why not? Even in World War One there were Germans and our blokes who stopped fighting in the trenches for Christmas. So, what do you reckon?'

Ellie almost smiled. She really liked the idea of a Christmas truce. She'd always liked to have a goal. And a short-term goal was even better. Doable.

'I reckon we should give it a shot,' she said. If soldiers could halt a world war for a little peace and goodwill at Christmas, she and Joe should at least make an effort.

He was watching her with a cautious smile. 'Can we shake on it?'

'Sure.'

His handclasp was warm and strong and, for Ellie, just touching him sparked all sorts of flashpoints. But now she had to find a way to stay calm. Unexcited. Neutral.

Her goal was peace and goodwill. For Christmas.

Their smiles were uncertain but hopeful.

But then, in almost the same breath, they both re-membered.

'Jacko,' they exclaimed together and together they hurried down the veranda to the lounge room.

There was no sign of their son, just his teddy bear lying abandoned on the floor near the empty cartons.

Ellie hurried across the room and down the hall-way to the kitchen. 'Jacko?' she called, but he wasn't there either.

Joe was close behind her. 'He can't have gone far.'

'No.' She went back along the hallway to the bed-rooms, calling, 'Jacko, where are you?' Any minute she would hear his giggle.

But he wasn't in his room. Or in her bedroom. Or in the study, or Nina's room. The bathroom was empty. A wild, hot fluttering unfurled in Ellie's chest. It was only a small house. There wasn't anywhere else to look.

She rushed back to the lounge room as Joe came through the front door.

'I've checked the veranda,' he said.

'He's not here.' Ellie's voice squeaked.

'He must be here. Don't panic, Ellie.'

She almost fell back into her old pattern, hurling defensive accusations. *How could you have left him?*

But she was silenced by the quiet command in Joe's voice, and by the knowledge that she'd been the one who stormed out.

'What was Jacko doing before you came outside to talk to me?' she asked with a calmness that surprised her.

'He was playing hide and seek with the bear. Here.' Joe swished aside the long curtain beside the door.

Ellie gasped.

Jacko was sitting against the wall, perfectly still and quiet, peeping out from beneath his blond fringe, hugging his grubby knees.

'Boo!' he said with a proud grin. 'I hided, Mummy.'

They fell on him together, crouching to hug him, laughing shakily. United by their mutual relief.

It wasn't a bad way to start a truce.

Dinner that night was leftover Spanish chicken. For Joe and Ellie the atmosphere was, thankfully, more relaxed than the night before, and afterwards, while Ellie read Jacko bedtime stories, Joe did kitchen duty, rinsing the plates, stacking the dishwasher and wiping the bench tops.

By the time he came back from checking the station's working dogs and making sure the chicken coop was locked safely from dingoes, Ellie was at the kitchen table, looking businesslike with notepaper and pen, and surrounded by recipe books.

'I need to plan our Christmas dinner menu,' she said, flipping pages filled with lavish and brightly coloured Christmas fare.

'I don't suppose I can help?'

She looked up at him, her smile doubtful but curious. 'How are your cooking skills these days?'

'About the same as they were last time I cooked for you.'

'Steak and eggs.' Her nose wrinkled. 'I was hoping for something a little more celebratory for Christmas.'

'Well, if you insist on being fussy...' He pretended

to be offended, but he was smiling as he switched on the kettle. 'I'm making tea. Want some?'

'Thanks.'

At least the truce seemed to be working. So far.

While Joe hunted for mugs and tea bags, Ellie returned to her recipe books, frowning and looking pensive as she turned endless pages. As far as Joe could tell, she didn't seem to be having much luck. Every so often she made notes and chewed on her pen and then, a few pages later, she scratched the notes out again.

'Our Christmas dinner doesn't have to be lavish,' he suggested as he set a mug of tea with milk and one sugar in front of her. 'I'm fine with low-key.'

'I'm afraid it'll have to be low-key. We don't have much choice.'

With an annoyed frown, Ellie pushed the books away, picked up the tea mug and sipped. 'Nice tea, thanks.' She let out a heavy sigh. 'The problem is, I didn't order a lot of things in for Christmas. Jacko and I were supposed to be spending the day with Chip and Sara Anderson on Lucky Downs. All they wanted me to bring was homemade shortbread and wine and cheese. But now, with the creeks up, we won't be able to get there.'

She waved her hand at the array of books. 'Some people spend weeks planning their Christmas menus and here am I, just starting. Yikes, it's Christmas Eve tomorrow.'

Joe helped himself to a chair and picked up the nearest book: *Elegant and Easy Christmas.*

'Those recipes are gorgeous,' Ellie said. 'But they all need fancy ingredients that I don't have.'

He flicked through pages filled with tempting pictures—a crab cocktail starter, turkey breast stuffed with pears and chestnut and rosemary, a herb-crusted standing rib roast, pumpkin and caramel tiramisu.

'I see what you mean,' he said. 'These are certainly fancy. Would it help if we make a list of the things you have in store?'

'Well, yes, I guess that's sensible.' Ellie rolled her eyes. 'I've a pretty good range of meat, but my problem is the trimmings. I don't have the sauces and spices and fancy herbs and that sort of thing. So I'm afraid we're stuck with ordinary, boring stuff. For Christmas!'

'Hmm.'

She looked up, eyeing Joe suspiciously. 'You're frowning and muttering. What does that mean?'

'It means I'm thinking.' Truth was—an exciting idea had flashed into his head. Crazy. Probably impossible.

But it was worth a try.

'Excuse me,' he said, jumping to his feet. 'I need to make a phone call.'

'There's a phone here.' Ellie nodded to the wall phone.

'It's OK. I've bought a sat phone, and I have the numbers stored.'

She looked understandably puzzled.

Adorably puzzled, Joe thought as he left the room.

By the light of the single bulb on the veranda, he found the number he wanted. Steve Hansen was an ex-Army mate and, to Joe's relief, Steve answered the call quickly.

'Steve, Joe Madden here. How are you?'

'I'm fine, Joe, heard you were back. How are you, mate? More importantly, where are you? Any chance of having a Christmas drink with us?'

'That's why I'm ringing,' Joe said. 'I've a huge favour to ask.'

'Well, ask away, mate. We both know how much I owe you. If it wasn't for you, I would have flown home from Afghanistan in a wooden box. So, what is it?'

CHAPTER SEVEN

MIDAFTERNOON ON CHRISTMAS Eve and the Karinya kitchen was a hive of activity.

At one end of the table, Ellie and Jacko were cutting shortbread dough into star shapes—with loads of patience on Ellie's part. At the other end, Joe, having consulted an elderly everyday cookbook, was stuffing a chicken with a mix of onion, soft breadcrumbs and dried herbs. To Ellie's amusement, he was tackling the task with the serious concentration of a heart surgeon.

By now the rain had stopped and the air was super-hot and sticky—too hot and sticky for the ceiling fan to make much difference. Flies buzzed at the window screens and from outside came the smell of once parched earth now turned to mud.

With the back of her hand, Ellie wiped a strand of damp hair from her eyes. She was used to hot Christmases and she'd come to terms with the ordinariness of this year's Christmas fare so, despite the conditions, she was actually feeling surprisingly upbeat.

She was certainly enjoying her truce with Joe.

And yet she was nervous about this situation. Playing happy families with her ex *had* to be risky. It was highly possible that she was enjoying Joe's company far too much. Already, today they'd caught themselves laughing a couple of times.

Surely that had to be dangerous?

Could laughter lead to second thoughts? Could she find herself weakening and becoming susceptible to Joe's charms, just as her mother had warned?

Then again, she knew these happy vibes couldn't last. By Boxing Day, she and Joe would be back to normal.

Normal and divorced and leading separate *peaceful* lives.

'OK,' she said briskly, whipping her attention from her broken marriage to her neat sheets of shortbread stars and her small son's not-so-neat efforts. 'I think it's time to pop these gourmet masterpieces into the—'

She stopped in mid-sentence as an approaching sound caught her attention.

Thump-thump-thump-thump-thump-thump-thump...

Jacko squealed. 'Heli-chopper!'

Joe looked up from his task of stitching the chicken and grinned. 'That's probably Steve.'

'Steve?' Ellie frowned as the roar of the chopper blades grew louder. Closer.

'Steve Hansen. A mate of mine from the Army. He got out last year.'

'Oh.'

In a heartbeat Ellie guessed exactly what this meant. Joe was no longer stranded here. She went cold all over. Joe had found an escape route. A friend with a helicopter was coming to his rescue. He was about to leave her again.

Ridiculously, she began to shiver in spite of the heat. *This* was the reason for last night's mysterious and secretive phone call. Joe had never explained, and all morning she'd been wondering.

Now, with an effort, she dredged up a smile. 'Well, that's *your* Christmas sorted.'

Joe looked at her strangely, but anything he might have said was drowned by the helicopter's noisy arrival directly above the homestead roof.

There'd been helicopters at Karinya before. They'd come to help with the mustering, so little Jacko wasn't frightened by the roaring noise. In fact he was squealing with delight as he dashed to the window.

The chopper was landing on the track beside the home paddock and, with a whoop of excitement, Joe picked the boy up and flipped him high onto his broad shoulders.

Ellie gulped. The sight of her son up on his father's big shoulders was...

Breathtaking...

'Are you coming to say hello to Steve?' Joe called to her before he hurried outside, leaving her with her arms akimbo and a table covered with raw chicken and unbaked cookies.

Ellie had no idea how long this interruption would take, so she found space for the uncooked food in the fridge.

By then, the helicopter had landed and Joe and Jacko were waiting at the bottom of the front steps until the blades stopped whirring. Jacko was jigging with excitement. Ellie's stomach felt hollow as she joined them.

It's OK. I'll be fine. Joe has to leave some time, and it's probably easier to say goodbye now, without going through the whole business of Christmas first.

Joe was grinning at her, his rugged face relaxed and

almost boyish with excitement. He looked a bit like Jacko. Or Jacko looked like him.

It wasn't a cheering thought now, when he was about to leave them. Ellie's heart did a sad little back-flip.

The rotor blades slowed. A door in the helicopter opened and a beefy red-haired pilot with a wide friendly grin appeared.

'Ho! Ho! Ho!' he called jauntily as he climbed down.

'Merry Christmas!' responded Joe and the two men greeted each other with handshakes and hearty back slaps. Joe's smile was wide as he turned back to Ellie and Jacko. 'Come and meet Steve. He was in Afghanistan with me, but he's set up in Townsville now and he's started his own chopper charter business.'

Pinning on her brightest smile, Ellie took Jacko's hand and encouraged him forward. 'Hi, Steve. Nice to meet you.'

'You, too,' Steve said warmly. 'Merry Christmas.' He shook hands with Ellie, then bent to ruffle Jacko's hair. 'Hello, young fella. You're a chip off the old block if ever I saw one.'

'This is Jacko,' Joe said proudly, adding a bright-eyed smile that included Ellie.

'Hi, Jacko.' Steve waggled his eyebrows comically, making the little boy giggle.

To Ellie, he said, 'I remember how excited Joe was when this little bloke was born. The news came through when we were all in the mess. You should have seen this man.' He slapped a big hand on Joe's shoulder. 'He was so damn proud, handing around his phone with a photo of his son.'

'How…how nice.' Ellie was somewhat stunned. She

glanced at Joe, saw the quick guarded look in his eyes, which he quickly covered with an elaborate smile.

'And now Jacko's a whole two years old,' Joe said.

'You're a lucky little bloke, Jacko,' announced Steve and then he nodded to the helicopter. 'And you're certainly in for an exciting Christmas.'

An exciting Christmas? Ellie frowned. What was this about?

She was struck by a ghastly thought. Surely Joe wasn't planning to take Jacko with him? 'What's going on?' she demanded.

Now it was Steve who frowned.

'Everything's fine, Ellie,' Joe intercepted quickly in his most soothing tone. 'Steve's brought out extra things for Christmas.' Turning to Steve, he said, 'I haven't told Ellie about this. I was keeping it as a surprise.'

'Ah!' Steve's furrowed brow cleared and was replaced by another grin. He winked at Ellie. 'Romantic devil, isn't he?'

Clearly Joe's Army mates didn't know about their divorce. Ellie found it difficult to hold her smile.

'Stand back then, Mrs Madden, while we get this crate unloaded.'

Dazed, she watched as Steve Hansen climbed back into the helicopter and began to hand down boxes and packages, which Joe retrieved and stacked on the ground.

There was an amazing array. Boxes, supermarket bags, wrapped parcels. A snowy-white Styrofoam box with *Townsville Cold Stores* stamped on the side.

As the last carton came out, Joe turned to Ellie with a complicated lopsided grin. 'I thought you deserved a proper Christmas. You know, some of the fancy things you were missing.'

She gave a bewildered shake of her head. 'You mean this is all fancy Christmas food? For me?'

'North Queensland's freshest and best,' responded Steve from the cockpit doorway. 'I set my wife Lauren on the hunt and she's one hell of a shopper.'

Ellie was stunned. 'Thank you. And please thank Lauren.' Again she was shaking her head. 'I can't believe you and your wife have gone to so much trouble, especially on Christmas Eve. It's such a busy time.'

Steve shrugged. 'Joe knew exactly what he wanted, and bringing it out here has been my pleasure.' He gave another of his face-splitting smiles. 'Besides, I'd do anything for your husband. You know Joe saved my life?'

'No,' Ellie said faintly. 'I didn't know that.' She hardly knew anything about Joe's time in the Army.

'Out in Oruzgan Province. Your crazy husband here broke cover to draw enemy fire. I was literally pinned between a rock and a hard place and—'

'Steve,' Joe interrupted, raising his hand for silence, 'Ellie doesn't need to hear your war stories.'

But Steve was only silenced momentarily. 'He's way too modest,' he said, cocking his thumb towards Joe. 'They're saying we're all heroes, but take it from me— your husband is a *true* hero, Ellie. I guess he's never told you. He risked his life to save mine. He was mentioned in despatches, you know, and the Army doesn't hand those out every day.'

'Wow,' Ellie said softly.

Wow was about all she could manage. The admiration and gratitude in Steve's eyes was so very genuine and sincere. She had difficulty breathing.

He risked his life to save mine.

But Joe obviously hadn't told Steve that he was now divorced, which made this moment rather confusing and embarrassing for Ellie, not to mention overwhelming. Her throat was too choked for speech. Her lips were trembling. She pressed a hand to her mouth, willing herself not to lose it in front of these guys.

'Thanks for sharing that, Steve,' she managed to say eventually. 'Joe never tells me anything about Afghanistan.' To keep up the charade, she tried to make this sound light and teasing—a loving wife gently chiding her over-protective husband.

'Well, it's been a pleasure to finally meet you and Jacko,' Steve said. 'But I'm afraid I have to head back. We're throwing a Christmas party at our place tonight. Pity you guys can't join us, but Lozza will have my guts for garters if I'm late.'

Already, he was climbing back into the cockpit.

Without Joe.

'You'd better hurry and get your things,' Ellie told Joe.

'My things?'

'You're not leaving without your luggage, surely?'

His blue eyes shimmered with puzzled amusement as he stepped towards her. Touched her lightly on the elbow. 'I'm not leaving now, Ellie,' he said quietly. 'I'm not going anywhere till the floods go down.'

'But—'

He cupped her jaw with a broad hand. 'Relax. It's cool.' His smile was warm, possibly teasing. His touch was lighting all kinds of fires. 'I couldn't let you eat all this stuff on your own.'

And then his thumb, ever so softly, brushed over her lips. 'Let's wave Steve off, and get these things inside. And then we can really start planning our Christmas.'

Our Christmas.

Joe was free to leave. Steve Hansen would have taken him back to the coast in a heartbeat—no questions asked. Instead Joe had *chosen* to stay.

And the way he'd looked at her just now was like the Joe of old.

But that was crazy. He couldn't... They couldn't...

She mustn't read too much into this. It was Christmas and Joe wanted to spend more time with Jacko. It was the only logical, believable explanation—certainly, the only one Ellie's conscience could accept.

But as Steve took off with the downdraught from his chopper flattening the grass and sending the cattle in the next paddock scampering, she had to ask, 'So, if you knew Steve could fly out here, why didn't you get him to rescue you?'

Joe shrugged. 'It would have been difficult, leaving the hire car stranded here.'

It was a pretty weak excuse and Ellie didn't try to hide her scepticism.

'Besides,' Joe added smoothly, 'you and I decided on a truce, and how can you have a truce between two people if one of the combatants simply walks away?'

As excuses went, this was on the shaky side too, but Ellie wasn't going to argue. Not if Joe was determined to uphold their truce. And not when he'd gone to so much trouble and expense to celebrate Christmas with her and Jacko.

'Come on,' he said, hefting the white box of cold stores. 'Let's see what Steve's managed to find.'

* * *

The packages were piled into the kitchen and it was just like opening Christmas presents a day early.

In the box from the cold stores, nestling in a bed of ice, they found the most fantastic array of seafood—export quality banana prawns, bright red lobsters, a slab of Tasmanian smoked salmon, even a mud crab.

'I may have slightly over-catered,' Joe said with a wry grin. 'But seafood always looks a lot bigger in the shell.'

In another cold bag there was a lovely heritage Berkshire ham from the Tablelands. This brought yet another grin from Joe. 'If the wet closes in again, we'll be OK for ham sandwiches.'

The rest of the produce was just as amazing—rosy old-fashioned tomatoes that actually smelled the way tomatoes were supposed to smell; bright green fresh asparagus, crispy butter-crunch lettuce, further packets of salad greens, a big striped watermelon. There were even Californian cherries, all the way from the USA.

In yet another box there were jars of mustard, mayonnaise and marmalade. Pickles and quince paste from the Barossa Valley. Boxes of party fun—bonbons and sparklers, whistles and glow sticks.

And there was a plum pudding and brandy cream, and a bottle of classic French champagne, and another whole case of wine of a much classier vintage than the wines Ellie had bought.

She thanked Joe profusely. In fact, on more than one occasion, she almost hugged him, but somehow she managed to restrain herself. Joe might have been incredibly, over-the-top generous, but Ellie was quite sure a newly ex-wife should *not* hug the ex-husband she'd so recently served with divorce papers.

It was important to remember that their Christmas truce was nothing more than a temporary cessation of hostilities—*temporary* being the operative word.

Ellie forced her mind to safer practical matters—like what they were going to do with the stuffed chicken and shortbread dough sitting in the fridge.

'We'll have them tonight,' suggested Joe. 'They'll be perfect for Christmas Eve.'

So the chicken and assorted roast vegetables, followed by shortbread cookies for dessert, became indeed the perfect Christmas Eve fare.

A cool breeze arrived in the late afternoon, whisking away the muddy aroma, so Ellie set a small table on the veranda where they ate in the gathering dusk, sharing their meal with Jacko.

Joe stuck coloured glow sticks into the pot plants along the verandah, lending a touch of magic to the warm summer's night.

Jacko was enchanted.

Ellie was enchanted too, as she sipped a glass of chilled New Zealand white wine, one of Joe's selections.

She had spent the past four years working so hard on Karinya—getting up at dawn, spending long days out in the paddocks overseeing the needs of her cattle, and then, after Jacko was born, fitting in as much time as possible to be with him as well.

Most nights, she'd fallen into bed exhausted. She'd almost forgotten what it was like to take time out to party.

Putting Jacko to bed on Christmas Eve was fun, even though he didn't really understand her explanation about the pillowslip at the end of his cot. He would soon work it out in the morning, and Ellie's sense of bubbling anticipation was enough enthusiasm for both of them.

When she tiptoed out of Jacko's room, she found Joe on the veranda, leaning on the railing again and looking out at the few brave stars that peeked between the lingering clouds.

He turned to her. 'So when do you fill Jacko's stocking?'

She smiled. 'I've never played Santa before, so I'm not exactly an expert, but I guess I should wait till I'm sure he's well and truly asleep. Maybe I'll do the deed just before I go to bed.'

'I'd like to make a contribution,' Joe said, sounding just a shade uncertain. 'I asked Steve to collect something for Jacko.'

'OK. That's nice. But you can put it under the tree and give it to him in the morning.'

'I'd like to show it to you now. You might want to throw it in with the Father Christmas booty.'

'Oh, there's no need—'

But already Joe was beckoning Ellie to follow him inside, into the study, where he promptly shut the door behind them.

'This makes a bit of a noise and I don't want to wake him.' He was trying to sound casual, but he couldn't quite hide the excitement in his eyes.

Intrigued, Ellie watched as he pulled a box from beneath the desk and proceeded to open it.

'Oh, wow!' she breathed as Joe drew out the world's cutest toy puppy. 'A Border Collie. How gorgeous. It looks so real.' She touched the soft, furry, black and white coat. 'It almost feels real and it's so cuddly. Jacko will love it!'

'Watch this.' Joe pressed a button in the puppy's stomach and set it on the ground. Immediately, it sat up and barked, then dropped back to all fours and began to scamper across the floor.

'Oh, my goodness.' Ellie laughed. 'It's amazing.'

The puppy bumped into the desk, backed away and then proceeded to run around in circles.

'I knew Jacko was too little for a real dog,' Joe said. 'But I thought this might be the next best thing.'

'It is. It's gorgeous. He'll be over the moon.' *The presents I bought won't be half as exciting.*

Joe was clearly pleased with her reaction. 'One of the guys in our unit bought a toy like this for his kid's birthday, and his wife put a movie of the boy and the puppy on the Internet. It was so damn cute it more or less went viral at the base.'

'I can imagine.' Ellie was touched by how pleased Joe looked, as if it was really important to find the right gift for his son.

'The other present I brought back with me was totally unsuitable,' he said. 'A kite. What was I thinking?'

'A kite from Afghanistan?'

Joe rolled his eyes to the ceiling. 'Yeah.'

'But their kites are supposed to be beautiful, aren't they?'

'Well, yes, that's true, and it's a national pastime for the kids over there, but a kite's not really suitable for a two-year-old. I just didn't think. I'll keep it for later.'

The puppy had wound down now and Joe scooped it up, unselfconsciously cradling it in his arms.

It wasn't only *little* boys who looked cute with toy dogs, Ellie decided.

'So you might like to put this in with the Santa stash,' he said.

'But then Jacko won't know *you* bought it for him.'

'That's not important.'

Ellie frowned. 'I think it is important, Joe. If you're going to go away again for ages at a time, a lovely gift like this will help Jacko to remember you.'

Perhaps this was the wrong thing to say. Joe's face turned granite-hard—hard cheekbones, hard eyes, hard jaw.

Silence stretched uncomfortably between them.

Ellie wished she knew what he was thinking. Was he regretting his decision to work so far away? Perhaps he felt differently about leaving Jacko now that he'd met the boy and so clearly liked him?

It was more than likely that Joe loved Jacko. For Ellie, just thinking about Joe heading off there to that freezing, lonely, big ocean made her arms ache strangely. They felt so empty and she felt sad for Joe, sad for Jacko too—for the tough, complicated father and his sweet, uncomplicated son.

Maybe she even felt sad for herself?

No. I've made my choices.

It seemed like an age before Joe spoke. 'I'd rather my son remembered *me*, not the toys I've given him.'

Ellie swallowed. It was hard to know whether he was taking the high moral ground or simply being stubborn. But he was sticking to his decision.

She held out her hand. 'In that case, I'd love to add this puppy to the Santa bag. Jacko will adore it. He'll be stoked.'

'You want to keep it in this box?'

'No. It looks more true-to-life out of the box.' Ellie hugged the puppy to her stomach. 'Joe, you haven't bought a Christmas present for me, have you?'

The hard look in his eyes lightened. 'There might be a little something. Why? Does that bother you?'

'Yes. I don't have anything for you. I never dreamed—'

He smiled crookedly. 'Chill, Ellie. It's no big deal. I know you haven't been anywhere near shops.'

Just the same, she was going to worry about this and it would probably keep her awake.

This is damn hard, Joe thought as Ellie left with the dog. Coming home was *so* hard. So much harder than he'd expected.

Of course, he'd always known he would have to make big adjustments. Soldiers heard plenty of talk about the challenges they would face as they transitioned from the huge responsibilities and constant danger of military life to the relative monotony and possible boredom of civilian life.

But Joe had been convinced that his adjustments would be different, easier than the other men's. To begin with, he wasn't coming home to a wife and family.

Or at least he hadn't planned to come home to a wife and family.

And yet here he was—on Christmas Eve—divorced on paper, but up to his ears in family life and getting in deeper by the minute.

He had to face up to the inescapable truth. No matter how much distance he put between himself and his family, there would always be ties to Ellie and Jacko.

It was so obvious now. He couldn't believe he hadn't seen it before.

And here was another thing. By coming back to Karinya, he was forced to see his absence in Afghanistan from Ellie's point of view, and he didn't like the picture he discovered.

While he'd played the war hero, earning his fellow soldiers' high regard, his wife—she'd still been his wife, after all—had slogged for long, hard days on this property, and she'd done it alone for the most part. As well, with no support whatsoever from him, she'd weathered the long awaited pregnancy and birth of their son.

On her own.

After the years of heartbreak and invasive procedures that had eroded their marriage, Joe knew damn well that the nine months of pregnancy must have been a huge emotional roller coaster for Ellie.

And what had he done? He'd tried to block out all thoughts of her pregnancy. And he'd let her soldier on. Yes, Ellie had most definitely *soldiered* on. Alone. Courageously.

Just thinking about it made Joe tremble now. During that whole time, Ellie must have believed he didn't care.

Hell. No wonder she had trouble trusting his motives today. No wonder she'd expected him to escape in Steve's chopper as soon as he had the chance.

And yet, strangely, escape had been the last thing on his mind. Shouldn't he be worried about that?

CHAPTER EIGHT

WHEN ELLIE WOKE early next morning, she felt an immediate riff of excitement, a thrill straight from childhood.

Christmas morning!

She went to her bedroom window and looked out. It was raining again, but not too heavily. She didn't mind about the rain—at least it would cool things down.

'Happy Christmas,' she whispered to the pale pink glimmer in the clouds on the eastern horizon, and then she gave a little skip. Rain, hail or shine, she was more excited about this Christmas than she had been in years.

Having a child to share the fun made such a difference. And this year they had all Joe's bounty to enjoy, as well as his pleasant company during their day-long truce.

The truce was a big part of the difference.

Don't think about tomorrow. Just make the most of today.

On the strength of that, Ellie dressed festively in red jeans and a white sleeveless blouse with a little frill around the neckline. When she brushed her hair, she was about to tie it back into its usual ponytail when she changed her mind and left it to swing free about her shoulders.

Why not? They might be in the isolated outback, but it *was* Christmas, so she threaded gold hoops in her ears as well, and sprayed on a little scent.

On her way to the kitchen she passed Jacko's room, but he was still asleep, still unaware of the exciting bundle at the end of his cot. He normally wouldn't wake for at least another hour.

As Ellie passed the open door of Joe's room, she glanced in and saw that his bed was made, so he was already up, too. She felt pleased. It would be nice to share an early morning cuppa while they planned their day together.

Maybe they could start with a breakfast of scrambled eggs and smoked salmon with croissants? And they could brew proper coffee and have an extra croissant with that new, expensive marmalade.

Joe might have other ideas, of course. He wasn't in the kitchen, however.

Ellie turned on the kettle and went to the doorway while she waited for it to come to the boil. Almost immediately, she saw movement out in a paddock.

Joe?

She crossed the veranda to get a better view through the misty rain. It was definitely Joe out there and he was bending over a cow that seemed to be on the ground.

Ellie frowned. Most of her pregnant cows had calved, but one or two had been late to drop. She hoped this one wasn't in trouble.

Grabbing a coat and Akubra from the pegs by the back door, she shoved her feet into gumboots and hurried down the steps and over the wet, slippery grass, dodging puddles in the track that ran beside the barbed wire fence.

'Is everything OK?' she called as she reached Joe.

He'd been crouching beside the cow, but when Ellie called he straightened. He was dressed as she was in a dark oilskin coat and broad-brimmed hat. In the dull grey morning light, his eyes were very bright blue.

Ellie had always had a thing for Joe's eyes. This morning they seemed to glow. They set her pulses dancing.

'Everything's fine,' he said. 'You have a new calf.'

And now she dragged her attention to the cow and saw that she had indeed delivered her calf. It was huddled on the ground beside her, dark red and still damp, receiving a motherly lick.

'Her bellowing woke me up,' Joe said. 'So I came out to investigate, but she's managed fine without any help.'

'That's great. And now we have a little Christmas calf,' Ellie said, smiling.

'Yes.' Joe smiled too and his gaze rested on her. 'Happy Christmas, Ellie.'

'Happy Christmas.' Impulsively, she stepped forward and kissed him lightly on the cheek.

He kissed her in reply—just a simple little kiss on her cheek, but, to her embarrassment, bright heat bloomed where his lips touched her skin.

Awkwardly, she stepped away and paid studious attention to the little calf as it staggered to its feet. It was incredibly cute, all big eyes and long spindly legs.

'It's a boy,' Joe said, and almost immediately the little fellow gave a skip and tried to headbutt its tired mum.

Ellie laughed, but the laugh died when she saw Joe's suddenly serious expression.

'I've been thinking about you,' he said. 'I never asked what it was like—when Jacko was born.'

She felt winded, caught out. 'Oh, God, don't ask.'

He was frowning. 'Why? Was it bad?'

You shouldn't be bothering with this now. Not after all this time.

'I know I should have asked you long ago, Ellie.' Joe's throat worked. 'I'm sorry, but I'd like to know. Was…was it OK?'

Even now, memories of her prolonged labour made her wince. She'd been alone and frightened in a big Townsville hospital, and she'd been unlucky. Rather than having the assistance of a nice, sensitive and understanding midwife, the nurse designated to look after her had been brusque and businesslike. Unsympathetic.

So many times during her twenty plus hours of labour, Ellie could have benefited from a little hand-holding. A comforting companion. But she wouldn't tell Joe that. Not now.

Especially not today.

She dismissed his concern with a wave of her hand. 'Most women have a hard time with their first.'

A haunted look crept into his eyes. 'So it was tough?'

OK, so he probably wouldn't give up without details. She told him as casually as she could. 'Almost twenty-four hours and a forceps delivery.'

She wouldn't tell him about the stitches. That would totally gross him out. 'It was all perfectly normal in the end, thank heavens, but it had its scary moments.'

Joe looked away. She saw the rise of his chest as he drew a deep breath.

'But it was worth it,' Ellie said softly. 'It was so worth every minute of those long hours to see Jacko.' And suddenly she had to tell Joe more, had to help him to see the joy. 'He was the most beautiful baby ever born, Joe. He had this little scrunched up face and dark hair. And he was waving his little arms. Kicking his legs. He had long feet, just like yours, and he was so amazingly perfect. It was the biggest moment of my life.'

You should have been there.

Oh, help. She was going to cry if she kept talking about this. Joe looked as if he was already battling tears.

It was Christmas Day. They should *not* be having this conversation.

Forcing herself to be practical, Ellie nodded to the new calf and its mother. 'I'll bring them some supplements later but, right now, I'm hanging out for breakfast. Are you coming?'

It took a moment for the furrows in Joe's brow to smooth. He flashed a scant, uncertain smile. 'Sure.'

'Let's hurry then. I'm starving.'

On the homestead's back veranda, Ellie pulled off her gumboots and removed her hat and coat. Joe shouldn't have been paying close attention. But, beneath the outdoor gear, she was dressed for Christmas in skinny red jeans and a frilly white top. Winking gold earrings swung from her ears and her dark glossy hair hung loose.

'So I was thinking scrambled eggs and smoked salmon?'

Breakfast? With his emotions running high, Joe's thoughts were on tasting Ellie's soft pink lips and hauling her red and white deliciousness close. He wanted to peel her frilly neckline down and press kisses along the delicate line of her collarbone. Wanted to trace the teasing seams of her jaunty red jeans.

Yeah, right, Brainless. Clever strategy. You'd land right back where you started with this woman. Ruining her life.

'Joe?'

He blinked. 'Sorry?'

With evident patience, Ellie repeated her question. 'Are you OK with scrambled eggs and smoked salmon?'

'Sure. It sounds—'

'Mummy!' cried a high-pitched voice from inside the house. 'Look, Mummy, look! A puppy!'

Ellie grinned. 'Guess we'll deal with breakfast in a little while.'

For Joe, most of Christmas Day ran pretty much to plan. Jacko loved his gifts—especially the little dog, and the colourful interlocking building set that Ellie had bought for him. The three of them enjoyed Ellie's leisurely breakfast menu, and Joe and Ellie took their second cups of coffee through to the lounge room where they opened more presents from under the tree—mostly presents for Jacko from their respective families.

Ellie loved the fancy box of lotions and bath oils and creams that Steve Hansen's wife had selected for her. And, to Joe's surprise, she handed him a gift.

'From Jacko and me,' she said shyly.

It was very small. Tiny, to be accurate. Wrapped in shiny red paper with a gold ribbon tied in an intricate bow.

'I know I said I didn't have anything for you, Joe. I meant I hadn't *bought* anything. This…this is home-made.'

Puzzled, he opened it and found a USB stick, a simple storage device for computers.

'I've put all Jacko's photos on there,' Ellie said. 'Everything from when he was born. I…um…thought you might like to—'

She couldn't go on. Her mouth pulled out of shape and, as her face crumpled, she gave a helpless shake of her head.

Dismayed, Joe dropped his gaze and stared fiercely at the tiny device in his hand.

'It'll help you to catch up on Jacko's first two years,' Ellie said more calmly.

But Joe was far from calm as he thought about all the images this gift contained. Two whole years of his son's life that he'd virtually ignored.

He saw that his hand was trembling. 'Thanks,' he said gruffly. 'That's—'

Hell, he couldn't make his voice work properly. 'I…I really appreciate this.'

It wasn't enough, but it was the best he could do.

They phoned their families.

'It's bedlam here,' Joe's mother laughed. 'Wall to wall grandchildren.'

'Jacko loves the picture books you sent, Mum. And the train set from his cousins. They were a huge hit.' The phone line was bad after all the rain and he had to almost yell.

'We miss you, Joe. And we're dying to meet Jacko, of course. Everyone sends their love. I hope you're having a nice day, darling.'

'We are, thanks. It's been great so far. Everything's fine.'

He and Jacko went into the lounge room and built a tall tower with the new blocks while Ellie phoned her mother. Joe had no intention of listening in, but she also had to speak loudly, so he couldn't help but hear.

'Harold gave you a diamond bracelet? How...how thoughtful. Yes, lovely. Yes, Mum, yes, Joe's still here. No, no. No problems...No, Mum. Honestly, you didn't have to say that. All right. Apology accepted. No, it doesn't mean I'm giving in. Yes, we're having beautiful seafood. One of Joe's Army mates brought it out in a helicopter. Yes, I thought so. *Very* nice. And Happy Christmas to you, too!'

Ellie came back into the lounge room and pulled a heaven-help-me face. 'I think I need a drink.'

'Right on time.' Joe grinned. 'The sun's well over the yardarm.'

They opened a bottle of chilled champagne and chose a CD by a singer they'd both loved years and years ago. And the music was light and breezy and the day rolled pleasantly on.

Jacko romped with his toy dog and played the new game of hide and seek, putting the dog behind cushions and then the curtains. Joe and Ellie made a salad with avocado, three kinds of lettuce and herbs. They set the dining table for lunch with the seafood platter taking pride of place. They added bowls for the crab shells and finger bowls floating with lemon slices.

They pulled bonbons that spilled rolled-up paper hats and corny, groan-worthy jokes. Jacko blew whistles and pulled crackers that popped streamers. The adults ate seafood and drank more champagne, while Jacko had orange juice and chicken. They laughed.

They laughed plenty.

Over plum pudding with brandy cream, while Jacko enjoyed ice cream with chocolate sprinkles, Joe told some of the funnier stories from Afghanistan. Ellie recalled the bush yarns the ringers had told around the campfire during last winter's cattle muster.

Joe couldn't drag his eyes from Ellie. She was glowing—and not from the wine. Her smiles were genuinely happy. Her dark eyes shone and danced with laughter. Even in an unflattering green paper hat, she looked enchanting.

And sexy. Dangerously so.

Seafood in the outback was a rare treat and she ate with special enthusiasm, sometimes closing her eyes and giving little groans of pleasure.

One time she caught Joe watching her. She went still and a pretty pink blush rose from the white frill on her blouse, over her neck and into her cheeks.

Watching that blush, Joe was tormented.

This truce was perilous. It was setting up an illusion. Messing with his head. Encouraging him to imagine the impossible.

After their long leisurely lunch, Ellie bundled a sleepy Jacko into his cot. The new black and white puppy, now named Woof, took pride of place next to his much-loved teddy bear. He was one very happy little boy.

On leaving his room, she found, to her surprise, that the dining table had already been cleared. Joe was in the kitchen and he'd cleared away the rubbish. He'd also rinsed their plates and glasses, and had almost finished stacking the dishwasher.

'Goodness, Joe. The Army's turned you into a domestic goddess.' *And a sex god*, she thought ruefully. *Or is it just too long since I've had a man in my kitchen?*

Grabbing the champagne bottle from the fridge, Joe

held it up with a grin. 'Want to finish this? There are a couple of glasses left.'

Ellie smiled. She was loving everything about this Christmas. 'It would be a crime to let those bubbles go flat.'

They took their glasses back to the lounge room. Outside, it was still drizzling and grey, but it was cosy inside with the coloured lights on the Christmas tree and a jazz singer softly crooning, and with Joe sprawled in an armchair, long legs stretched in close-fitting jeans and a white open-necked shirt that showed off his tan.

Ellie thought, *I'm almost happy. I'm so close to feeling happy that I can almost taste it.*

She *might* have been completely, unquestionably happy if this truce were real and not a charade.

It was scary—*super*-scary—to be having second thoughts, to wish that she and Joe could somehow time-travel back into their past and right a few wrongs. OK, right a *mountain* of wrongs.

It wasn't going to happen, of course. This pleasant and charming interlude was nothing more than time out. Time out for Christmas. From reality.

It was important to remember that. Ellie planned to make sure she remembered it. She hadn't needed her mother's phone call to remind her.

Joe hoped he looked relaxed, but it was getting harder and harder to stay cool and collected while Ellie kicked off her shoes and made herself comfortable on the sofa.

She arched and stretched like a sleepy cat and then sank against the cushions, offering him an incredibly attractive view of her long legs in slinky red jeans. She wriggled her bare toes and sipped champagne with a smile of pure bliss.

The urge to join her on the sofa was a major problem.

And here was an inconvenient truth.

Ellie was the only woman Joe had ever truly wanted and, despite the bitterness and sorrow that had blown apart their marriage, the wanting was still there. Had never really left. It was an involuntary, visceral, inoperable part of him. And right now it was—

Driving him crazy.

Ellie took another sip of her champagne and held the glass up to the light, admiring the pale bubbles. Then she looked at Joe and her gaze was thoughtful, almost...

Wistful?

He held his breath. It was so hard to sit still when all he wanted was to be there on the sofa with her, helping her out of that frilly blouse.

Almost as if she could read his thoughts, Ellie's smile turned wary. Colour warmed her cheeks again and her eyes took on a new heightened glow. She shifted her position, and Joe wondered if she was feeling the same fidgety restlessness that gripped him.

His head was crammed with memories of making love to her. He could remember it all—the sweet taste of her kisses, the silky softness of her skin, the eager wildness of her surrender—

'So,' Ellie said with an awkward little smile, 'how would you like to spend the afternoon?'

She was joking, right?

'Are you interested in watching a DVD?'

'Might be dangerous,' Joe muttered.

'A DVD? Dangerous?'

He pointed to the positioning of the TV screen. 'We'd have to share that couch.'

Ellie looked startled, as well she might. She tried to cover it with a laugh. 'And that's a problem?'

'When you're wearing those tempting red jeans—yes, a big problem.'

Her expression switched from startled to stunned. And who could blame her? It had probably never occurred to her that her ex still had the hots. For her.

Joe grimaced.

Ellie simply sat very still, clutching her champagne flute in two hands, staring at him with a hard to read frown.

To his surprise, she didn't look angry. Or sad. Merely bemused and thoughtful.

His heart pounded. What was she thinking? If she showed the slightest hint that she was on the same wavelength, he would be out of this chair…

Then Ellie dropped her gaze to her glass and ran a fingertip around its rim. 'That's part of our problem, isn't it?'

Joe waited, unsure where this was heading.

'There's always been an attraction.' Ellie swallowed, gave a self-conscious shrug. Kept staring at her glass. 'But perhaps we would have been better off if we'd spent more time talking. I know you hate getting too deep and meaningful, Joe, but I don't think we ever spent enough time just talking, did we?'

'Not without arguing, no.'

'Have you thought about it very often?' She looked away and swallowed nervously. 'Have you given much headspace to what went wrong for us?'

'Some.' Joe's throat was so tight he could barely speak. 'Yes.'

Ellie drained her champagne and set the glass on the coffee table. 'I must admit I don't like failing or giving up, so I've given quite a bit of thought to our problems since you left. Too much, I guess.'

'What conclusions have you come to?'

Ellie regarded him with a narrowed, doubtful gaze. 'I can't imagine you'd really want to talk about this now.'

'No, it's OK. Go on. I'm listening. I'd actually like to hear your point of view.'

She seemed to think about this for a moment and then suddenly dived in. 'Well, I've always thought we were like that old song. Married in a fever. One minute we were the world's hottest lovers. Next, we were trying to set up a cattle business and start, or I should say restart, our family.'

'And then it all got so hard.'

'Too hard,' Ellie agreed with a frown. 'And that's when we didn't talk enough. Or when we tried to talk we just ended up yelling.'

Joe nodded, recalling the distressing scenes he'd tried so hard to forget.

'But there's one thing I'm very grateful for, Joe. Even in the heat of it, you never raised a finger to hurt me.'

'I wouldn't. I couldn't.'

Ellie had tears in her eyes now. 'But I think, in the middle of it all, we somehow lost sight of each other.'

'Or maybe we never really took the time to know each other properly.'

'Yes, that too.' She looked down at her hands and rubbed at a graze on her knuckle. She sighed heavily.

'But, as I said the other day—it's probably not helpful to dredge up the past.'

Joe wasn't so sure. Already he could see evidence of how they'd both changed. When they were married, a conversation like this would have landed them square in the middle of another argument.

He had to admit he'd avoided over-thinking their past. It was easy in the Army to be completely distracted by the demands of an ever present, very real and life-threatening enemy. He'd lived from day to day, from task to task. It was simple—and necessary—to focus on the present and to block out his emotions, including any guilt regarding Ellie.

Now, it was hard to believe he'd been so single-minded. Some would call it pig-headed.

Selfish.

But had he anything more to offer Ellie now? He'd like to think that time and distance had honed the raw edges and given him maturity.

Watching him, Ellie gave an uneasy sigh, then pushed out of the couch and got to her feet. She walked to the window and peered out. 'It's stopped raining,' she said dully.

A kind of desperation touched Joe. She was walking away, changing the subject. And yet he had the feeling they'd been drawing close to something important. He'd even wondered if it was something they both wanted, but were too afraid to reach for.

He edged forward in his seat, his mind racing, trying to balance his gut instincts with cool reason.

At the same moment, Ellie spun away from the window. 'Oh, stuff it! I think I *do* need to talk about this. I mean, it's our only chance. Once you're gone—'

She lifted her hands as if she felt lost. Helpless.

Joe's chest tightened. This was a *huge* moment and he suddenly knew that he wanted to grab it with both hands. Even so, he felt nervous—as nervous as he had in Afghanistan crossing a field laced with landmines.

'I'm happy to talk,' he said carefully. 'I mean—we're in a kind of now-or-never limbo at the moment, so perhaps we should make the most of it.' He chanced a smile. 'And we do have the protection of a truce.'

Slowly, cautiously, Ellie returned his smile, and then she walked back to the sofa and sat at one end, straight-backed, lovely, but clearly nervous. 'Where should we start?'

Good question. 'I'm open.'

Ellie squinted her dark eyes as she gave this some thought. 'Maybe we could start with the whole Army thing. There's so much I don't really know about you, Joe. Not just what you've done as a soldier since we split. I never really understood why you wanted to join the Army in the first place—apart from a chance to escape.'

'Well, I was planning to join the Army before I met you.'

'Yes, I knew that. But why, when your family own a cattle property? Don't you like cattle work?'

'Sure. I like working on the land.' Joe knew he could say this honestly. He loved the physical demands, loved being at one with the elements, loved the toughness and practicality required of people in the bush. 'But with four older brothers, I had very little say in how things were run at home. So the idea of the Army was more an act of rebellion than anything.'

Ellie looked surprised.

'I was fed up with being bossed around by those brothers of mine. They were always giving me orders. Not just on the property either. They loved telling me what I should and shouldn't do with my life. I decided, if I was going to be bossed around, it may as well be for a damn good reason and not simply because I was the runt of the litter.'

'Some runt,' she said with a smile.

'That's how I felt.'

Her smile was sympathetic. 'There was an age gap between you and the rest of your brothers, wasn't there? What was it? Six years?'

'Almost seven. I think they hoped I'd stay at the homestead and be a mummy's boy, but I wasn't staying home when they were off having adventures. So I was always trailing after them like a bad smell, trying to keep up. Annoyed the hell out of them, of course.'

'Not great for the self-esteem.'

Joe gave a shrug. 'I eventually came into my own, but not until boarding school. By then, all my brothers had left and, as far as my classmates were concerned, I wasn't anyone's little brother. I was just Joe Madden.'

'Football star.'

'For a few years, yeah.'

'And the Army was a bigger and more exciting version of boarding school?'

This time Joe chuckled. 'You missed your calling. You should have been a shrink.'

But Ellie was frowning again, as if she was lost in thought. 'I *still* think the Army provided an excellent excuse to escape when our marriage got too rough.'

'You're probably right.' He fingered a loose thread

in the upholstery on his chair. 'Maybe it was something I had to get out of my system.'

'Is it out of your system now?'

That was a damn good question. 'I think so. I've certainly no ambition to become an old soldier.' Joe looked up and met her gaze. 'So what about you, Ellie?'

To his surprise, she looked suddenly trapped. 'How do you mean?'

'If we're spilling our guts, I thought you might have something about you and your family that we've never outed.'

'I was an only child,' she said quickly. Almost too quickly. 'No sibling issues for me.'

But the shutters had come down. Everything about her was instantly defensive.

Joe waited. Ellie had never really explained why she'd left home straight after high school and moved to Queensland. He knew her dad had died when she was young and her relationship with her mum was OK, but not close, certainly not as close as Angela would have liked. There were issues, he was sure.

'I thought we were talking about you and the Army,' she said stiffly.

Ohhh-kaaay. Closed door.

Joe wasn't prepared to push Ellie on this. Not today. 'So we're back to me.' He shrugged. 'So, what else would you like to know?'

'Are you glad you joined up?'

The question was loaded, and Joe did his best to skirt it. 'The Army has its good points and I've certainly gained new skills.' He smiled. 'And not all of them involve blowing things up.'

More relaxed again now, Ellie picked up a cushion

and hugged it to her chest. Joe told himself he could not possibly be jealous of a cushion.

'So do you feel OK after everything you've seen and done over there?'

'Are you asking if I have post-traumatic stress?'

'Well, you seem fine, but there's so much talk about it. I wondered.'

'Well, I certainly feel OK, and I came out with a clean psych test. Perhaps I was lucky.'

'I guess you were due some good luck.' Her expression was a little sad. 'Just the same, do you think being a soldier has changed you at all?'

Joe hesitated, remembering the rockiest days of their marriage and the times he'd retreated when he'd known Ellie needed him. He'd watched his wife sink deeper into despair and it had felt like a knife in his heart, but he'd had no idea how to help her. At the time, he'd been completely inadequate.

'I'd like to think I've changed,' he said. 'I've certainly had to shoulder some hefty responsibilities.'

Ellie nodded slowly. 'It shows. I think it's given you confidence. You seem much surer of yourself now.'

This assessment caught him by surprise, especially as the smile that accompanied it was warm and tender.

Careful, Ellie.

When she looked at him like that, he was back to thinking about rolling with her on that couch.

CHAPTER NINE

JOE HAD THAT look again.

The look stole Ellie's breath and sent heat licking low, making her uncross and recross her legs, making her think too much about his powerful body, hidden by that snowy white shirt and blue jeans. He had that look in his eyes that made her forget all the warnings she'd given herself and wish for things she had no right to wish for.

She sat up straighter, and Joe watched with an attentiveness that did nothing to ease the edgy distractedness of her thoughts.

Talk, Ellie. This conversation's been going well. Don't lose it now.

'So,' she said quickly before she lost her nerve, 'I guess we agree that our relationship might have been more successful if we'd taken things more slowly at the start. We might have understood each other better if we'd talked more. Been a bit more tolerant.'

Joe nodded, but then his eyes took on a wicked teasing gleam. 'Then again, I'm not sure it was possible for us to go slow.'

She felt her cheeks glow.

'The way I remember it, we were pretty damn impatient,' Joe went on, clearly ignoring her discomfort.

This was *not* a helpful contribution, even though it was true. Right from the start, they hadn't been able to keep their hands off each other.

'At least we're managing to behave ourselves now,' she said tightly.

'We're divorced, Ellie.'

Clunk.

'Yes. Of course.' But she felt winded, as if he'd carelessly tossed her high and then left her to fall.

She slumped back against the cushions and closed her eyes while she waited for her heartbeats to recede from a frantic gallop to an only slightly less frantic canter. When she opened her eyes again, Joe was still watching her, but his expression was serious now.

'Just so I'm clear,' he said quietly. 'You're not having second thoughts, are you? About the divorce? About us?'

Second thoughts?

No, surely not. The very idea made her panic. She had her future planned. Joe had his future planned. They had their separate lives planned.

She couldn't have regrets. There was no point in trying to turn the train wreck of their marriage into a fairy tale.

And yet...

Had Joe really opened a door?

Was *he* having second thoughts about their marriage? And their divorce?

He was looking a tad winded, and Ellie could well believe that he'd shocked himself with his question.

It was too much to take in, sitting down. She launched

off the sofa and onto her feet again, and began to pace while her mind spun like a crazy merry-go-round.

'Second thoughts?' she repeated shakily. 'I don't think so, Joe.'

And yet...

And yet...

Her sense of loss was a dull ache inside her, and every time she looked at Joe now the pain grew sharper.

'But I...I don't know for sure.' She shot him a quick, searching glance. 'What about you?'

His throat worked and he tried for a smile and missed. 'I was good with our settlement. But...but if you wanted to reconsider it—'

Ellie stopped pacing. *Oh, God. This was not supposed to happen.*

'It was all decided,' she whispered. 'I've filed for divorce. I've served you with the papers. You've signed them.'

'I know. I know. And don't panic, Ellie. Nothing has to change.'

'No.' She took a deep breath, and then another.

'Unless...' Joe added slowly, carefully. 'Unless we want it to change.'

Whoa!

He was opening up a choice.

He was actually making her an offer. A second chance to right their wrongs.

Ellie's heart soared high with hope, then hovered, trembling with fear, terrified of failure. How could they possibly make this work?

'It can't be wise, can it?'

'Does it feel unwise?'

'No.' She stared at him anxiously. 'I don't know.'

'I guess we can only trust our own judgement.'

'Trust. That's a biggie. And…and now there's Jacko to consider as well. I'd hate to stuff things up for him.'

'It's the last thing I'd want, Ellie.'

She was swamped by an urge to simply rush into Joe's arms, to have done with the what-ifs and the wherefores and to simply give in to her burning need to have his arms about her, his lips working the magic she could so well remember.

I have to be sensible.

More than any other time in her life, she had to be cautious and unimpulsive and prudent.

'How can we be sure we won't just make the same mistakes?' But, even as she asked this, she knew the answer. After everything she'd been through, there were no guarantees. From the point of conception, every stage of life was a calculated risk.

After four years in the Army, Joe would know this, too.

'I guess we could avoid our first mistake,' he said. 'We could try taking things slowly, spending time together, getting to know each other again.'

'Just talking? Just friends?'

'It's only a suggestion.' Joe was out of his chair now and he was pacing too, as if he was as restless as she was.

It wasn't a sitting-down kind of conversation.

'What about this job you have lined up?' Ellie challenged. 'Chasing pirates or poachers or whatever?'

'The agency probably wouldn't be thrilled if I pulled out at the last minute, but I'd be prepared to.'

Ellie reached the bookcase and turned. Half a room separated them now. 'So if we tried this, how would it work? Would you be living here, at Karinya, and help-ing me with the cattle?'

'Yes, just as I was before, I guess.' He smiled at her. 'But hopefully without the arguments.'

'Or the sex.' Ellie's pacing came to an abrupt halt.

Her gaze met Joe's and she saw his eyes blaze with a look of such fierce intensity that her breathing snagged.

It wasn't possible, was it?

She and Joe couldn't live together and simply be friends. She was practically climbing the walls after just a few days of having him here, touching close and yet out of reach. And now they were planning to extend this condition indefinitely.

As if they were both frozen by the prospect, they stood, poised like opponents at Wimbledon, both as tense as tripwires, both breathing unevenly, with the stretch of carpet an unpassable gulf between them. Their no-go zone...

Help.

All Ellie could think about was crossing that space, rushing into Joe's arms and sealing her lips to his. Winding her limbs around his tree trunk body. Kiss-ing him senseless.

Say something, Joe. Break the spell.

He didn't move, didn't speak, and something inside Ellie—most probably her willpower—snapped.

She flew across the carpet.

'I'm sorry,' she murmured half a second before her lips locked with Joe's.

But Joe wasn't looking for an apology, not if the hungry way he returned her kiss was any guide. He pulled her close, held her close, keeping her exactly where he wanted her, hard against him in all the right places, while his lips and tongue worked his dazzling, dizzying magic.

He tasted of Christmas and champagne and all kinds of happiness, and Ellie was swooning at the long-remembered taste and smell and intensely masculine feel of him.

Her knees gave way, but fortunately her hands linked behind his neck provided a timely, but necessary anchor.

If there were warning voices shouting in her head, she didn't hear them. She was drowning in a whirlpool whipped to urgency by years of loneliness and heart-break and a longing she could no longer deny.

I'm sorry, Joe. I've been trying so hard to forget you, but I can't. I've missed you so much.

So, so much.

The hunger in his kisses was reassuring. Wrapped in his arms with their wild hearts beating together, she could feel the passion in him...both thrilling and com-forting, as if they'd both arrived at the same place and knew it was where they were meant to be.

Everything about Joe felt familiar yet even more ex-citing than before. Especially now when, in the smooth-est of manoeuvres that Ellie didn't stop to analyse, he swung her off her feet and onto the sofa.

Cushions tumbled as their bodies tangled, urgency ruling the day. Joe kissed her chin, her earlobe, her throat, and her skin leapt to life wherever he touched. In no time he was peeling down the neckline of her blouse, trailing downward kisses that grew hotter and hotter.

Ellie helped him with the buttons. The blouse fell away and Joe released a soft groan. In a haze of need, she might have groaned too. She wanted his touch. Wanted it more than air.

'Mum! Mamma!'

Oh, help.

They stilled as if they'd been shot. Hearts racing, they stared at each other in disbelief.

'Mummy!' came another imperious summons from the little bedroom down the hallway.

Ellie was panting slightly. She was straddling Joe, flushed and half-dressed.

Joe looked into her eyes and smiled, his eyes hinting at dismay warring with amusement. 'His master's voice,' he said softly.

A shaky sigh broke from Ellie.

'Mummee!' Jacko called again and the cot was rattling now.

Joe reached for her, a hand at her nape, easing her down towards him. He kissed her gently, taking his time to sip at her lower lip. 'Saved by our son,' he murmured.

Our son. Not the kid or the boy. *Our* son.

'I don't feel saved.'

'No, you feel damn sexy.' He skimmed broad hands over bare skin at her waist, inducing a delicious shiver. 'At least we've made interesting progress.'

Indeed. Already, as they eased apart, Ellie sensed a new light-heartedness in Joe.

But that wasn't supposed to happen.

'I'll get Jacko,' he offered, rising to his feet while she began to re-button her blouse.

'Thanks.'

A moment later, Ellie heard his cheerful greeting and Jacko's delighted crow in response. She went to the bathroom and found a hairbrush, studied her reflection in the mirror. Her skin was flushed and glowing, her hair a messy tangle.

They'd come so close…

So close.

But had they been taking an important step, as Joe hinted, or had they teetered on the brink of a huge mistake?

And, more to the point, if they went ahead with their plan for a second chance, could she make it work? Could she be a better partner now?

When she thought about the woman she used to be, too anxious and heartbroken and self-absorbed to see beyond her own problems, she cringed.

She wanted to be so much better.

Was fate pushing her to grab this new chance?

A freak of nature, a flooded river, had brought Joe back into her life, but, just now on the sofa, they'd been gripped by a passion that revealed a deeper truth. They couldn't deny the attraction was still there. Stronger than ever.

It was still hard to believe that they might retrieve their marriage. For so long Ellie had thought of herself as already divorced. It wouldn't be easy to start again. They'd both have to make big adjustments. Huge. But if Joe was willing…

She wanted to give it her very best shot.

Joe lifted Jacko from the cot and took him to the bathroom and then to the kitchen for a drink and a snack, but he was working on autopilot. His mind was on Ellie and the big step they'd just taken. The choice they'd made.

The choice *he'd* made.

Sure, impulsive physical need had played a part, just as it had when he'd first met Ellie. But when he'd married her he hadn't really had a choice. He'd made his girlfriend pregnant and he'd felt a strong obligation to 'do the right thing' by her.

Again, four years ago, when he was so clearly making Ellie unhappy, he'd felt obliged to set her free. He hadn't known any other way to handle their problems and at the time, he'd convinced himself he had no other choice, although, as Ellie had correctly pointed out, he'd also been escaping.

Today, however, he'd had choices.

He had a signed legal document setting him free and he had a job to go to, a safe escape route. He had plenty of options.

But he'd also learned, after only a few days here, that he and Ellie had both changed during their years apart. Sure, they'd been on vastly different journeys—there couldn't be two experiences more different than war and motherhood—but they'd both matured as a result.

And, of course, they now had Jacko. Within a matter of days Joe loved the boy with a depth that he'd never dreamed possible. As for Ellie...

He knew now that he'd never stopped loving Ellie. He'd walked away from her when it all got too difficult and he'd buried his pain beneath the façade of a hardened soldier, but the bare truth was—his feelings for her were still as tender and loving as they'd been at the start.

So, yeah, he had loads of choices now.

And today he'd chosen to stay.

With Jacko between them, they spent the afternoon taking a tour of inspection around Karinya. Ellie carted nutritional supplements to the new mothers and calves, and she showed off her investments to Joe—two new dams and a windmill pump—as well as her successful experiments with improved pastures.

'You've done an amazing job,' he kept saying over and over.

They visited his favourite haunts, including the old weathered timber stockyards and the horse paddock. Together, they leaned on the railings, feeding carrots and sugar cubes to the horses that came to greet them, while Jacko played at their feet with a toy dump truck, filling its tray back with small rocks and then tipping them out.

'I think I should apologise,' Ellie said, needing to give voice to the issue at the forefront of her thoughts. 'I can't believe we decided on a set of rules and I immediately went crazy and broke them.'

'Have you heard me complaining?' Joe asked with a smile.

'But we didn't stick to the plan we'd made five minutes earlier.'

'Maybe it wasn't a very good plan. Not very realistic, at any rate.' Covering her hand with his, Joe rubbed his thumb over her knuckles. 'Don't start worrying, OK?'

Ellie smiled. 'OK.' There was something so very reassuring about this new confidence of Joe's. And, if she wanted this to work, she had to learn to trust him, didn't she?

Back in the ute, they drove on. They checked the river height and found that it was going down. In another day or two it would be crossable. But there was no more talk of Joe leaving.

Instead, happy vibes arced between them. A delicious anticipation whispered in the afternoon air. As they drove back to the homestead, they shared smiles and gazes over the top of their son's snowy head, gazes that shimmered with hope and excited expectation.

For their evening meal, Joe carved the Christmas ham with great ceremony and they ate thick, delicious pink slices piled on sourdough bread and topped with spicy mango chutney. Dessert was a cheese platter, plus extra helpings of Christmas pudding, and there was another bottle of Joe's delicious wine.

After dinner, to Jacko's squealing delight, the three of them played hide and seek together in the lounge room. Then they piled onto the sofa, with Jacko on Joe's knee, and together they read his new picture books. Ellie and Joe made the appropriate animal noises—Joe was the lion, the cow and the bear, while Ellie was the monkey, the duck and the sheep—and Jacko copied them, of course, amidst giggles and gales of laughter.

While Joe supervised Jacko's bath time—a rather noisy affair involving submarines and dive-bombing planes—Ellie took care of the dishes and tidied the kitchen. They put Jacko to bed.

And then, at last, they were alone.

Ellie was a tad self-conscious as they settled in the lounge room, enjoying the last of the wine. She was on the sofa and Joe was in the armchair again, but she knew they shared expectations about the night ahead. She was plucking up the courage to raise the question of sleeping arrangements. Surely Joe wouldn't stay in Nina's room tonight? Was it up to her as his hostess to mention this?

Despite this minor tension, their mood was relaxed. Music played, low and mellow. The tree lights glowed. They talked about their little boy—about the miracle that he was and how cute and clever—even which boarding school he might attend in the distant future.

Then, almost as if he could hear them, a little voice called, 'Drink o' water, Mummy.'

With a roll of her eyes, Ellie put down her glass and went to the kitchen to fill Jacko's cup. When she took it in to him, he only wanted two sips.

'Nuff,' he said, shaking his head.

'This is just a try-on,' Ellie scolded gently. 'Now snuggle down.' She kissed him. 'Time for sleep. Night, night.'

Jacko snuggled, closed his eyes and looked angelic. Satisfied and pleased, Ellie returned to the lounge room.

'Where were we?' she said to Joe.

'I believe we were congratulating ourselves on our wonderful son.'

They laughed together softly, so as not to disturb him.

Then Jacko wailed again. Ellie waited for a bit, but the wailing grew louder and, when she went to his room, she saw that he'd thrown his teddy bear out of the cot. Of course, she picked it up and gave it back to him. 'No more nonsense. It's bedtime,' she said more sternly.

Back in the lounge room, Joe was flicking through a magazine. Ellie settled on the sofa once more, picked up her glass.

'Joe!' came an imperious summons from the bedroom. 'Joe! Joe!'

Ellie sighed. 'He's overexcited.'

'Too much hide and seek after dinner?'

'Possibly. This happens from time to time.'

'So how do you usually handle it?'

'Depends. Sometimes Nina—'

'Nina?'

'The nanny.'

'Oh, yes, I forgot about her. When's she due back?'

'After New Year. Anyway, sometimes we let Jacko cry and he just gives up after a bit.'

Joe frowned at this.

'It's acceptable parenting, Joe. It's called controlled crying. We've never let him cry for *very* long.'

He still looked disapproving. 'Perhaps I should go in there and try speaking to him sternly?'

'Like a sergeant major?' Ellie sent him an *as if* look.

'A little fatherly discipline.'

'Are you sure you know how to reprimand a two-year-old?'

'I can only try.'

She shrugged. 'At this time of night, anything's worth a try.' But, suddenly unsure, she added quickly, 'Don't be too hard on him, Joe.'

Despite her last minute doubts, Ellie's gaze, as she watched Joe leave the room, was one of pure lust and feminine admiration. She was prepared to admit it now—Joe Madden had always been the most attractive guy she'd ever met, and now he was hotter than ever.

It wasn't just the extra muscle power. There was a new confidence and inner strength in him that showed in the way he held himself. And it was there in his gorgeous smile. In his attitude, too. He'd certainly taken fatherhood in his stride.

Actually, this last surprised her. Back in the bad old days when they were having so much trouble starting their family, Ellie had always been worried that Joe's heart wasn't really in the project—that parenthood was more her goal than his. Heaven knew she'd accused him of this often enough in the past.

Now, she heard Jacko's delighted greeting as Joe reached him, and she listened with keen interest for the 'stern message' he planned to deliver.

She was steeled for the gruff voice, followed by Jacko's whimpering cry. Telling Jacko off wouldn't work, of course. Almost certainly, she would have to go in there and soothe her little boy.

The house remained hushed, however, and all Ellie heard was the low rumble of Joe speaking so quietly that she couldn't hear the words. And then silence.

The silence continued.

Ellie finished her wine and the CD came to an end. She didn't bother to replace it. She was too absorbed and curious about the lack of sound down the hallway.

Eventually, it got the better of her and she tiptoed to the door of Jacko's room.

In the glow of the night light, she saw Joe by the cot and Jacko lying on his tummy, eyes closed, his long lashes curling against his plump cheeks. Joe was patting his back gently and patiently.

Ellie smiled. So much for the firm fatherly reprimand.

Sensing her presence, Joe looked up and lifted his free hand to halt her. Then he touched a finger to his lips and the message was clear. *I'm in charge here and everything's under control.*

Fascinated, she propped a shoulder against the doorjamb and waited, while Joe continued his gentle patting regime with surprising tenderness and patience. It was hard to believe this big tough man had just returned from a war that involved blowing things up and quite probably killing his enemy.

After another minute or so, Joe lifted his hand carefully from Jacko's back. Ellie waited for the boy to do his usual trick of wriggling and squirming till the patting resumed.

But Jacko remained peaceful and still and, a moment or two later, Joe came out of the room.

His smile was just a tad smug.

Safely back in the lounge room, Ellie narrowed her eyes at him. 'So that was your stern father act, huh?'

Joe grinned. 'Worked a treat.'

'You old softie.'

'That's one thing I'm not.' He touched her elbow. 'Come here and I'll prove it.'

Heat rose through Ellie like a flame through paper. Without hesitation, Joe drew her in.

And just like that she was in his arms and he was kissing her, hauling her closer still. And, of course, his boast was accurate. There was nothing soft about this guy, apart from his lips. The rest was hard-packed manly muscle and bone from head to toe.

The house was silent as they kissed.

And the silence continued. The only sound was the far-off call of a curlew in the trees along the river.

Joe took Ellie by the hand and led her to the darkened doorway on the far side of the lounge room, and the question about the night's sleeping arrangements became irrelevant.

This was the bedroom he knew well, the room they'd once shared.

They didn't bother with lights. The glow of the

Christmas tree reached where they stood at the foot of the bed, as they shared another kiss, another embrace.

Now their kisses were long and leisurely and sweet. They'd been denied this for so long, never believing it could happen. But despite the four years' separation, they lingered now on the brink, confident and trusting, savouring the exquisite anticipation.

Joe kissed Ellie's neck and she kissed his rough jaw. His lips brushed over her lips, once, twice in teasing, tantalising, unhurried caresses.

He lifted her chin to trace her jaw line with his lips. 'I've missed you, Ellie.'

'Me too. I've missed you so much.' She hadn't admitted it before, but she wanted him to know. 'The whole time you were away, I was terrified you'd be killed. There'd be stories about Afghanistan on the news, and I always had to turn them off.'

Tears threatened, but she didn't want to cry. Instead she sought pleasure, easing his shirt from his jeans and slipping her hands beneath, rediscovering the texture of his skin, the hair on his chest.

Her hands dipped lower and a soft sound broke from Joe, and next moment he was undressing her and she was loosening his clothes as best she could.

She had a brief moment of panic. 'I'm not the same, Joe. Since the pregnancy and everything, things have—'

'Shh.' He silenced her with his kiss as his hands cupped her less than perky breasts. 'You're lovely, Ellie,' he murmured against her lips. 'Beautiful. I'm still crazy about every little part of you.'

He melted the last of her fears as he guided her to the bed—the bed they'd shared till four years ago. And now, still, they took their time, making love slowly, tenderly, with whispered endearments and heartbreaking thoroughness.

They knew each other so well, knew all the ways they longed to be touched and kissed and roused—a knowledge they alone shared—intimate truths that lay at the heart of their marriage.

This night wasn't just about sex and wanting—it was a time-honoured act of love, where past hurts could begin to heal and glimmers of hope for their future dawned.

Afterwards they lay close together, talking softly in the moon-silvered dark.

'Welcome home,' Ellie said.

She felt Joe's smile against her neck. 'It's good to be back.'

'We have to make it work this time.'

Gently he lifted a strand of hair from her cheek. 'We will, Ellie.'

She turned, admiring his strong profile limned by moonlight. 'I love the way you're so confident now.'

'Older and wiser perhaps...'

'That should apply to me too then.'

'I'm sure it does.'

Ellie suspected that she'd changed, too. She was also more confident, more willing to believe in a happy future. But was she prepared to trust?

I must. It's important...

'At least we no longer have the whole baby thing hanging over us.'

Joe shifted away slightly, as if he needed to see her face. 'I assume with everything you've been through that you're content with just one?'

'Oh heavens, yes. Aren't you?'

'Absolutely. I'm perfectly content with the three of us.' He chuckled. 'Anyway, I doubt we could improve on Jacko.'

Ellie smiled at the obvious pride in his voice, but of course she agreed. They couldn't hope for more than their cute little guy, even if they were able to, which they weren't.

'So we're OK not using precautions?' Joe asked.

'Well, yes, we must be, surely. Look how hard it was to get Jacko.' Ellie frowned. 'But I will check with the doctor next time I'm in town. Another pregnancy is the last thing I'd want now when we're starting over. I'm more than happy to close that chapter in my life.'

'That's fine by me.'

Unexpected relief flowed through Ellie. That particular ordeal was behind them. They'd been tested in the fire and were stronger now. 'So we should be OK, shouldn't we?'

'I reckon we should be very OK.'

As if to prove it, Joe kissed her again, deep and hard and long.

Melting fast, she wound her arms around him, and they made love again with a new sense of giddy freedom and joyful abandon.

CHAPTER TEN

BOXING DAY MORNING dawned. As always, Ellie woke early, and the first thing she saw was Joe lying beside her. She indulged in a few secret moments to drink in the sight of him, so dark and manly and downright hot, and her heart performed a little joyful jig.

She went to the kitchen and made tea and when she brought two steaming mugs back to bed Joe was awake.

'I can't lie around having tea in bed,' he protested. 'I've a cattle property to run.'

'Humour me, Joe. Just for today. It's a public holiday. I know that doesn't mean much out here, but let's pretend.'

Ellie opened the French windows onto the verandah and plumped up the pillows and they sat in bed together, looking out over Karinya's paddocks, where bright new tinges of green were already showing after the recent rains.

She clinked her tea mug against his. 'Here's to us.'

'To us,' he agreed, dropping a kiss on her brow.

'That's assuming you're still happy to stay.'

'Of course I am, Ellie.'

Joe shot her a wary sideways glance. 'You've got to trust me, you know. This won't work if you don't.'

'I know.' She was surprised he'd pinpointed the heart of her problem. She was learning to trust—to trust not just Joe, but herself, even to trust in their ability to face the unknown future. 'I'm sorry,' she said.

'And no more apologies. We could spend a lifetime apologising to each other, but we've got to put the past behind us.'

Ellie nodded and sipped at her tea. 'We're going to have to tell Jacko that you're his daddy.'

Joe looked so happy at this he brought tears to her eyes. She was quite sure he would have hugged her, if they hadn't been holding mugs of scalding tea.

After a while, she said, 'It wasn't all bad before, was it?'

Joe shook his head. 'To be honest, I have more good memories than bad ones.'

She settled deeper into the pillows, pleased. 'Do you have a favourite memory?'

'Sure,' he said with gratifying promptness. 'It would have to be that day you brought dinner out to the Lowmead paddock.'

'Really?'

'Yeah. I'd had a hell of a time, trying to fix that bore. It took me hours and hours in the blazing heat. And, just as I finally got on top of it, you turned up with a big smile and all this fabulous food.'

Ellie felt a little glow inside, just watching the way Joe smiled at the memory.

'You brought me soap and a towel,' he said. 'And, while I was cleaning up, you set up the picnic table and chairs under a tree. There was a red checked tablecloth and you'd cooked up this fabulous curry, and we had chilled wine, and caramel rum pie for dessert.'

'So it's true, after all?' She gave him a playful dig with her elbow.

'What's that?'

'The way to a man's heart is through his stomach.'

Joe chuckled. 'Guess it must be.' He picked up her hand, threaded his fingers with hers. 'That day's a standout because it was so spontaneous.'

'Spontaneous for you. I'd had it all planned for days.'

'A brilliant surprise. We were so relaxed and happy.'

'We were,' she agreed.

'So what's your favourite good memory?'

'Oh, I think it has to be the night we almost slept in the car park.'

'But ended up in the bridal suite?'

'Yes. It was just such fabulous fun.'

'Especially as we'd never had a proper honeymoon. We'll have to go there again some time.'

Ellie lifted a sceptical eyebrow. 'Do you think they'd welcome Jacko?'

'My mother would babysit.'

'Well, yes, that would be nice.' But Ellie's chest tightened at the mention of Joe's mother. She was reminded of her mother. She drew a quick calming breath. 'I suppose we're going to have to tell our families, aren't we?'

'About us?'

'Yes.'

'My folks will be delighted.'

'Mine won't.'

For the first time that morning, Joe frowned.

'It's OK.' She kissed his lovely stubbled jaw. 'Mum's going to have to cop it sweet. If she doesn't, I'm not going to let it bother me.'

'Promise?'

'Promise.'

* * *

The transition into their new lifestyle was surprisingly smooth. The river levels went down and neighbours who were travelling to Charters Towers offered to drive Joe's hire car.

Joe rang to resign from his new position patrolling the Southern Ocean. At New Year, Joe and Ellie both rang their families with their news and, as they'd predicted, Joe's parents were delighted.

'Joe, darling, I'm so relieved,' his mother cried. 'I've been praying for this.' She was tearful on the phone, but she was laughing and excited through her tears. 'Just wait till I tell your father. He'll be thrilled. As you know, we're dying to meet Jacko. And to see Ellie again. Do you think you'll be able to visit us soon? But if it's too difficult, perhaps we could visit you? We have so many extra hands to help here. It would be easier for us to get away.'

Before Ellie could ring her mother, there was a call from Nina, the nanny.

'Ellie, I'm so sorry to leave you in the lurch, but I've just had the most amazing job offer. It's my dream—a position at the Cairns Post.'

Ellie knew Nina had studied journalism and that the nanny job had only ever been a fill-in. 'Don't worry,' she said with a serenity that surprised her. 'My husband's back from the Army, so we'll manage between us.'

She hadn't told Nina about her plans to divorce Joe, so the girl accepted his return as a perfectly normal and lovely surprise.

Of course, Ellie had been looking forward to having a nanny so that she could be free to join Joe in the outdoor work that she enjoyed so much, but Joe was much keener to share both the housework and the yard work than he'd been in the past, so she knew that she'd spoken the truth. They'd sort something out between them.

They'd arrived at a new calmness, a new sense of closeness and solidarity. It truly did feel as if they'd been through a long and painful trial and come out the other side stronger. And, as a reward, it seemed they'd been granted their fairy tale ending, and Ellie was beginning to trust that it really could last this time.

Although her phone call to her mother tested her newfound confidence.

'Oh, Ellie, I knew it! You're as weak as water when it comes to that man.' Her mother's voice was shrill with dismay. 'I don't expect it will be very long before he leaves you again.'

Ellie made an effort to argue in Joe's defence, but her mother showed no signs of relenting.

'Do you really think you're helping me, Mum, by getting stuck into Joe every chance you have?'

Her mother spluttered. 'I'm only thinking of you, dear.'

'I don't think so.'

'But Ellie—'

'You've been down on Joe ever since you met him.' Actually, that wasn't quite true. Her mum had been suitably charmed by Joe the first time she'd met him. It was only later, around the time of their wedding, that her attitude seemed to have soured. Ellie had never understood why.

'It's not just my opinion, Ellie. Harold warned me about Joe.'

'Harold?'

'Yes. He's learned so much from local politics and he's a very astute judge of human character. But you've always been so sure you know better. I don't suppose you'll visit us now, will you?'

'Well, I—'

'We'll just have to come and visit you then.' This was announced snappily before her mother hung up.

Ellie wasn't given an option. Her mother and Harold were coming, steamrollering their way into her home.

The very thought made her feel fragile and nervous. She tried to shrug it off. She told herself that, with Joe on her side now, she was strong enough for anything.

She almost believed this until the morning she realised that her period was two weeks late.

CHAPTER ELEVEN

S<small>HE COULDN'T BE</small> pregnant, surely?

The sudden fear that gripped Ellie was all too familiar. She was remembering the miscarriage that had started the downhill spiral and had ultimately wrecked their marriage.

Even the memories of Jacko's safe delivery couldn't calm her. Everything from Jacko's conception to his birth had been carefully controlled under strict clinical supervision. Ellie had spent most of the nine months of her pregnancy in Townsville while a manager took care of the cattle and Karinya.

An unplanned pregnancy now would bring to the surface all her old anxieties, all the tension and worry about another possible miscarriage or ongoing complications.

The last thing she wanted was to go through that again. Not now she had Jacko, and she and Joe were so happily reconciled.

Everything was going so well. Joe was genuinely pleased to be back here, to be with her and to be working Karinya. Only last night he'd told her this again.

'After growing up on a cattle property, I can't help feeling attached to the land—to the red dirt and the mulga. I'm scratching my head now, wondering how on earth I thought I'd be happy floating around in the Southern Ocean without you and Jacko.'

But would Joe still be happy if their old problems surfaced?

Ellie was aware of the irony of her new dilemma—she'd spent so many years longing for a baby, and now she was dismayed by the prospect. She and Joe had negotiated their new future together based on the understanding that their fertility and pregnancy issues were behind them.

They were starting a new life—just the three of them.

I can't be pregnant. Not with my record. It must be just out of kilter cycles.

She hunted around at the back of the medicine cabinet and found a pregnancy testing kit—years old, but never opened. Fingers crossed, it would still work.

She was so nervous she thought she might throw up as she waited for the result to show. She closed her eyes, not brave enough to watch what was happening to the stick, and she prayed that two coloured lines would *not* appear.

I can't be pregnant. I can't.

She allowed longer than the allotted time, just to be sure, and then she opened her eyes the tiniest crack, and peeked nervously at the tiny screen.

Two lines.

Oh, my God. Two strong, thick, no-doubt-about-it lines.

This couldn't be happening. Sweat broke out on her forehead, her arms, her back.

She stared at the lines in a disbelieving daze. She knew she *should* feel happy about this, but she could only feel shocked and scared. And foolish.

Pregnancy would land her right back where she and Joe fell off the rails. They would be reliving that horror stretch. They'd have to go through all that uncertainty again.

Why on earth had she been so confident that this couldn't happen?

How could I have been such a fool?

Her hands were shaking as she wrapped the testing stick in a tissue and hid it in the rubbish bin. She put the second stick back in its box in the cupboard. She might try again in a few days' time, just to double-check, to make sure this wasn't a crazy mistake. Until then, she wouldn't tell Joe. She *couldn't* tell Joe.

There was no need to upset him unnecessarily, especially when his parents were due to visit them at the end of the week.

Stay Zen, Ellie.

She nailed on a smile, knowing that her major challenge now was to make sure that neither Joe nor Jacko could sense how tense she was.

Over the next few days, Ellie thought she managed quite well, but there was still no sign of her period. She tried again, and the second testing stick showed another pair of very strong lines.

Her tension mounted. Joe's parents would be arriving at the weekend and she'd been looking forward to their visit. She hoped they would see for themselves how happy she and Joe were now, and she'd been in a frenzy of preparations, setting up an extra bed in the spare room, cleaning and polishing, baking cakes and slices.

Now, she was going to have to tell Joe about the pregnancy before they arrived, and she really had no idea how he'd react. In the near future, she would need to see a doctor, too. That thought made her even more anxious.

On the night before the Maddens were due, Ellie's stomach was churning as she went to say goodnight to Jacko. Joe was reading him his favourite picture books—they'd been taking it in turns lately—but she'd spent longer than usual in the kitchen tonight, putting the final touches to her baking.

It was time to call a halt to the reading or Jacko would be over-excited.

She'd thought Joe was reading the books on the sofa, but the lounge room was empty. There was a light in the bedroom—no voices though, no growling lions or gibbering monkeys. Surprised, Ellie crossed quickly to the bedroom doorway.

The sight she found there stole her breath.

Her husband and son were sound asleep, lying together on top of the quilt. Joe had one arm stretched out and Jacko was huddled close, sheltered by his shoulder.

They looked so peaceful, so close. Father and son...

There was something so silently strong and protective about this simple scene. It touched a chord deep within her.

In the past few weeks she'd been growing more and more confident that, whatever happened, Joe was here to stay. Now, watching him sleeping beside his son, she felt a strong new soul-deep level of certainty.

With Joe she could face the future. They had everything they'd ever wanted right now, and they could cope with this pregnancy together, whatever the outcome.

I'll definitely tell him about the baby tonight, she decided. She would run a nice relaxing bath and, when she came to bed, she would wake Joe gently and tell him about the pregnancy. She would tell him so calmly that he'd know she was OK, that their marriage—no matter what happened—was going to be OK...

Ellie was smiling as she tiptoed away. The only dark cloud on her horizon was the prospect of Harold arriving with her mother in a fortnight's time. But she wouldn't think about him tonight, wouldn't let him spoil her calm and upbeat mood.

She ran a lovely warm bath, lit a rose-scented candle and placed it on a stool in the corner of the bathroom. She turned out the main light and the room was pretty in the soft glow of candlelight. Deliberately, she made herself relax and lie back, eyes closed, breathing slowly, deeply and evenly, in and out.

She pictured herself serenely and confidently telling Joe her news—not too excited and not at all anxious. She would be positive and optimistic, taking this new pregnancy in her stride.

The candle scents and the soft light were soothing. She sank a little lower into the warm, welcoming water. No matter what happened in the next few weeks, she would do everything to remain calm. For Joe. She would—

The phone rang in the kitchen.

Ellie sat up quickly. Joe was asleep. She wondered if it had woken him, or whether she should clamber out of the bath and run, dripping, through the house.

Then she heard Joe's footsteps crossing the lounge room and going down the hall. Heard his voice.

'Hello, Angela.'

Her mother.

Whoosh. Ellie sank beneath the water, incredibly relieved that Joe was dealing with this call. She couldn't handle a conversation with her mum tonight. It would only wind her up again, wiping out the Zen.

She certainly didn't want to think about two weeks of Harold in her house—and with only one bathroom. How many times might he accidentally open the door?

This ghastly thought wouldn't go away. It wrecked Ellie's peace and brought her sitting up so abruptly that water sloshed over the side of the bath. How on earth could she kid herself that baths were relaxing?

Without warning and totally against her will, she was reliving those nights when Harold came in. The images were still disgustingly vivid in her memory.

Harold's leer. His teeth flashing in his red face as he grinned at her. His eyes bulging as he stared at her breasts.

Ellie shuddered and squirmed, her skin crept and her relaxation was obliterated in a flash. It was useless to continue lying in the bath with memories of her step-father intruding. She stood quickly and scrambled over the side, not caring about the dripping water. She pulled the plug and the bathwater began to gurgle noisily down the plughole and along the old-fashioned plumbing.

As she reached for a towel, she thought she heard another sound beyond the gush of the disappearing water—the faint creak of the bathroom door opening. *Creepy Harold.*

She spun around.

Irrational fear exploded in her chest.

A shadowy male figure hovered in the doorway.

'Get out!' she screamed in a hot streak of panic. *'Get out!'* Her reaction was visceral, erupting from a place beyond logic. Eyes tightly shut, she screamed again. 'You monster. Leave me alone!'

'For God's sake, Ellie.'

She was so gripped by blinding panic it took a moment to come to her senses.

Joe?

Joe was standing at the door?

Of course it was Joe.

And he was staring at her in horror, as if she'd turned into a multi-headed, fire-breathing monster.

I'm sorry.

Ellie was panting and too breathless to get the words out at first. She tried again. 'I'm sorry, Joe, I—'

But he didn't wait for her apology. He took another glaring look at her, gave a furious shake of his head, then whirled around and left her, slamming the door behind him.

Appalled, shaken, Ellie sank onto the edge of the bath.

She couldn't believe she'd reacted like a maniac in front of Joe, as if she was terrified of her husband, the man she loved. It wasn't as if they hadn't shared the bathroom before. Only last week they'd had all kinds of steamy fun making love in the shower.

And she couldn't believe this had happened tonight of all nights, when she'd been trying her hardest to remain calm.

Clearly, she was as tense as a loaded mouse trap.

The look on Joe's face had said it all. She'd seen his stark despair, his disappointment and disgust.

She wanted to rush after him, but common sense prevailed. She would have a much better chance of offering a calm, rational explanation if she wasn't dripping wet and wrapped in a towel. Hastily she dried her body, her arms and legs and roughly towel-dried her hair.

Her silk kimono was hanging on a hook behind the door and she grabbed it quickly, thrusting her arms into the loose sleeves and tying the knot at the waist. As she dragged a comb through her wet hair, her reflection looked pale, almost haggard.

Too bad. She didn't have time to fuss about her appearance. She had to find Joe. The way he'd looked at her just now had frightened her badly.

It was as if he'd wanted to put as much distance between them as possible, as if he was certain their marriage was doomed, as if he'd already left her.

She didn't find him in the lounge room, or the kitchen, or the study, or their bedroom.

Had he left already? Taken off into the night?

Fearing the worst, Ellie hurried out onto the dark front veranda. Joe wasn't standing at the railing as she'd hoped.

Then she saw a shape on the front steps. She felt a brief flutter of relief until she realised that Joe was sitting slumped forward, as if defeated, with his head in his hands.

He looked shattered.

Her tough, highly trained, Special Forces soldier was sunk in total despair.

I've done this to him.

Ellie could feel her heart breaking.

She pressed her hand against the agonising ache in her chest. Now, more clearly than ever, she was aware of the depth of her love for Joe. These past few weeks had been the happiest in her life. The two of them were conscious of how close they'd come to losing each other and each new day together had felt precious. They'd even been laughing again, the way they had when they first met. And with Jacko joining in the fun, their lives had been so joyous. So complete.

Or had it all been a fragile mirage?

Had this bitter end always been waiting for them, hovering just around the corner?

After her hysterics in the bathroom, how could she possibly tell Joe about the pregnancy? How could she expect him to believe she'd cope with it calmly?

How could he have any faith in her?

Ellie was almost afraid to disturb him now, but she knew she had no choice. She had to try to apologise and to explain. Perhaps she even had to finally tell him about Harold.

Wasn't it time for courage at last?

Speaking to Joe was the first step.

Her legs were unsteady as she moved forward, her bare feet silent on the veranda floorboards.

'Joe?' she said softly.

His head jerked up. Instantly, he glared at her. 'What the hell's going on, Ellie?'

'Joe, I'm so sorry.'

Already he'd sprung to his feet, as agile as a panther. But his face was white in the moonlight. 'What's got into you?' He threw up his hands. 'What was that all about in there?'

'I'm sorry. It wasn't a reaction to you, Joe. Please believe me. I didn't know it was you.'

His scowl was derisive. 'Who else would it be, for God's sake? You saw me. I was standing right in front of you and you kept screaming. I'm your husband, damn it, not an axe-murderer. I thought—'

He shook his head and his lip curled in disgust. 'I

thought we were going to be OK, and then you go and pull a crazy stunt like that.'

'It wasn't a stunt.'

'What was it, then?' His eyes were fierce. 'You must have been truly terrified. Of what? Me? Am I supposed to find that reassuring?'

'I thought... For a moment, I thought...' Ellie swallowed the rising lump of fear that filled her throat. 'I can't explain unless I tell you...' The fear was stifling. 'There's...there's something I should have told you years ago.'

Joe stared at her, his blue eyes narrowed now—puzzled and mistrustful.

Ellie knew he must be wondering why she still had an apparently important issue that she hadn't shared with him. It probably made no sense at all after the soul-searching depth of their recent conversations.

'So, what is it?' he asked cautiously.

Despite the trembling in her stomach, Ellie came down the steps till she was next to him.

'It's Harold,' she said.

'Your stepfather?'

Ellie nodded.

Joe was frowning. '*He* freaks you out?'

'Yes.' It was all she could manage.

For long, nerve-racking seconds, Joe stared at her. She could see a muscle jerking in his jaw, betraying his tension, and she could see his thoughts whirring as he put two and two together. She saw the moment when understanding dawned.

He swore softly. 'That's why you left home so young?'

'I had to get away.'

Joe swore again with extra venom. He stood, glaring off into the black silent night, and when he turned to Ellie again, his eyes were still harsh, still uncertain.

'You've never breathed a word of this.'

'I know. I always meant to.'

'Why? Why couldn't you tell me?'

'I tried, but it was unbelievably hard. I felt so ashamed. And I'd already tried to tell my mother and she wouldn't believe me, so I thought I should just try to forget it, to put it all behind me.'

'Oh, Ellie.' Joe reached for her then. He took her hands, folded them in his, and then he slipped his arm around her shoulders and drew her close and his warm lips brushed her forehead. He sighed, and she felt his breath feather gently against her cheek.

It was the most wonderfully comforting sensation. Ellie dropped her head against his shoulder, savouring his strength. It felt so good to have offloaded this at last. And Joe understood. She should have known he would. She should have trusted him…

Then Joe said, 'Tell me now.'

Instinctively, she flinched. 'But you've already guessed.'

'My imagination's working overtime. I want to know the real story.'

'You might think I'm making a whole lot of fuss about nothing.'

'Nothing? After you almost clawed my eyes out to-night?'

She gave a defensive little shrug. 'I wasn't that bad.'

'Bad enough. And, whatever happened, I know it's affected you—it still affects you after all these years.' He gave her shoulder an encouraging rub. 'I'm not going to doubt you, Ellie.'

She knew this was true. Joe wasn't like her mother; she'd been blinkered and so impressed with her new role as the mayor's wife that she hadn't wanted to hear anything bad about Harold.

Joe, on the other hand, was genuinely worried—about her.

And so she told him.

They sat together on the wooden step, looking out over the dark, silent Karinya paddocks, where the only sound was the occasional soft lowing of a cow. Ellie's kimono fell open, exposing her knees, but she didn't worry about covering them, and she told Joe her story, starting with some of the things he already knew, like her father's death just before her thirteenth birthday, and how her mum had sold their farm and moved into town, marrying Harold Fowler eighteen months later.

'But, right from the start, Harold gave me the creeps,' she admitted.

She went on to explain how he'd just patted her at first, but over the next couple of years his attention had become more and more leering and suggestive, and then he'd come into the bathroom without knocking, choosing nights when her mother wasn't home.

She explained how she'd tried unsuccessfully to tell her mother.

'I knew then that if I stayed at home, the situation would have only got worse.' Ellie shuddered. 'And tonight I was thinking about Harold coming to stay here for two whole weeks. I don't suppose he'd dare to do anything stupid out here, but I was lying in the bath tonight, remembering, and wondering how on earth I would cope, and then the bathroom door opened and… and I freaked.'

Joe had listened to everything without interrupting, but now he said, 'Actually, he's not.'

Ellie frowned. 'Pardon?'

'Harold's not coming here. That's what I was coming in to tell you. Your mother phoned. She sounded a bit upset, but she usually does when she's talking to me. She was ringing to tell you that she's coming out here on her own. Harold's too busy to get away, tied up with council meetings or something.'

Ellie let out a loud huff of disbelief.

'And it's just as well he's not coming,' Joe said, clenching his fists on his knees. 'I might have felt obliged to take him outside and read him his horoscope.'

She almost smiled at this. 'I wonder if he guessed.'

'I reckon he knows I'm not his biggest fan. I haven't liked to say too much to you, but I've never taken to that guy.'

'And I should have told you about this long ago.'

Joe shrugged, then he looked at her for long thoughtful seconds before he spoke. 'It's interesting that you're not hung up about sex.'

Ellie gave him a shy smile. 'Not with you, at any rate.'

'Thank God.'

'But I think I probably have trust issues. I'm always expecting to be disappointed.'

'You've had your share of disappointments.'

'But I've reacted badly too. It probably sounds crazy, but I'm wondering if my father dying had an effect as well as Harold. I was always scared you were going to leave me.'

'And then I did leave.'

'And who could blame you?' Ellie's throat ached

as she looked away, remembering all the times she'd lashed out at Joe, blaming him unfairly, even though he couldn't possibly have been responsible for all her disappointments. She'd never really known where that unreasonable anger had sprung from. 'I guess I should have had some kind of counselling.'

'It's not too late.'

'No, but I already feel better, just having told you.'

Joe drew her in for another hug and, with her head against his shoulder, she closed her eyes, absorbing his warmth, his strength, his love.

Quietly, almost gently, he asked, 'So, while we're here, I guess I should ask if there's anything else you need to get off your chest?'

Oh.

Of course there was.

Ellie's nervousness shot to the surface again and she sat up straight, pulling away from him. She drew a deep breath. 'Actually, yes, I'm afraid there's something else quite important.' Her throat tightened and she swallowed, trying to ease her nervousness. 'There's another reason I've been tense, although I'm sure I'm going to be OK.'

Of course he looked worried, but he was trying to hide it. 'You're not sick, are you?'

'No, no. I'm fine. But—' Ellie dragged a quick steadying breath '—according to *two* home tests, I'm…I mean *we*…are…'

His face was in shadow so she couldn't see his expression, but she knew he was staring at her. Staring hard.

'You're *pregnant*?' he asked so softly it was almost a whisper, an incredulous whisper.

'I'm afraid it looks that way, if the home tests are accurate. They're a bit out of date, but the lines were very clear.'

This confession was met by a troubling silence. Ellie hugged her knees, not daring to guess what Joe might be thinking.

At last she had to ask, 'Are you OK, Joe?'

'Yeah, I'm OK, but I'm worried about you. How do *you* feel about this?'

It was a much better response than she'd feared.

'I'm getting used to it. Slowly. It was a horrible shock at first. I was so sure I was safe.'

'You had me convinced it couldn't happen.'

'I know. I'd convinced myself.' She hugged her knees more tightly still.

'How long have you known?'

'A few days. Since Monday. I hope you don't mind that I kept it to myself. I didn't want to bother you if it was a false alarm.'

Joe was staring at her again, and it was some time before he spoke. 'Wow.'

'Wow?'

'Yeah. I'm seriously impressed, Ellie.'

This was the last—the very last—reaction she'd expected.

'You've been worrying,' he said. 'I know you must have been. I know what a big deal another pregnancy is for you, and yet all week I had no idea you were worried about a thing. You've just carried on calmly, getting ready for my parents' visit as if nothing was the matter.'

'Well, I made a decision, you see. I'm going to stay calm about this pregnancy, whatever happens.'

Joe was smiling as he slipped his arm around her again. 'Good for you.'

Relieved beyond belief, Ellie leaned in and pressed a kiss to the underside of his jaw. 'I'll be upset if I lose another baby, of course I will, but you're the most important thing in my life now. You and Jacko. I've learned my lesson. I'm not going to let anything spoil what I already have.'

Reaching for Joe's hand, she pressed her lips to his knuckles. She still couldn't get enough of touching and kissing him.

'I love you, Ellie Madden,' he murmured against her hair.

'I know it's hard to believe from the way I behaved, but I've never really stopped loving you.'

'I can't believe I nearly let you go.'

'I can't believe I pushed you away.'

A hush fell over them and Ellie guessed they were both thinking how close they'd come to losing each other permanently.

'But we're going to be fine now,' Joe said.

'We are,' she agreed with absolute certainty.

'And I hope, for your sake, that this pregnancy's a breeze, Ellie, but, whatever happens, I promise I'll be there for you.'

Joe touched her cheek, turning her face to his. 'This time, and for ever, I'll be with you every step of the way.'

He sealed his promise with a kiss and it was, without doubt, their happiest, most heartfelt kiss ever.

EPILOGUE

Sunlight streamed through stained glass windows onto massive urns of white lilies and gladioli and carnations, the legacy of a big Townsville society wedding that had been held in the church on the previous day.

This morning, after the main service, a smaller group gathered around the font. Most of the Madden family were present, including Joe's parents. One of his brothers had been required to stay back to look after the property, but the other three were present, plus their wives and a flock of Joe's nephews and nieces.

Ellie's mother, Angela, was there too, smiling and looking genuinely happy for the first time in many months.

The past year had been an extremely distressing and difficult ordeal for Angela, but her separation from Harold and their subsequent divorce were finally behind her.

Now she was already settled in Townsville in a beautifully appointed penthouse apartment with stunning views of Cleveland Bay and Magnetic Island. After the christening, all the gathered friends and family were going back there today for a celebratory barbecue lunch on the rooftop terrace.

The new apartment was in Angela's name, but the mortgage was her ex-husband's responsibility. Of course, she'd taken him to the cleaners. After suffering unbearable public humiliation when gossip about his harassment of several young women had spread like wildfire through their country town, it was the least Angela could do—especially when she'd realised, to her horror, that the accusations her daughter had made all those years ago were true.

But all that was history now and today's gathering was an extremely happy occasion. Ellie looked radiant in a rose-pink linen dress that showed off her newly slim figure. In her arms, plump baby Will slept like a dream, blissfully unaware that he was wearing a long, intricately smocked christening gown edged with handmade lace that had been worn by members of the Madden family for over a century.

Will's older brother Jacko couldn't understand why a boy had been dressed in girl's clothes, although Jacko had learned quite quickly that babies were strange creatures who slept too much and cried a lot and demanded far more than their fair share of attention.

Today, however, Jacko was also in the limelight, as he was being christened alongside baby Will. Ellie had been too busy when Jacko was a baby to think of such things as christenings. These days, however, she was taking every aspect of motherhood in her stride.

There had only been one scary incident during the early months of this pregnancy when Joe had rushed her in to the hospital in Charters Towers, but, fortunately, it had been a false alarm. After a few days, she'd been allowed home again and, after that, everything had gone smoothly.

Will was an easy baby, who liked to sleep and eat and smile. His birth had not caused any dramas. He'd arrived just before dawn on a beautiful September morning, and Joe was with Ellie for every precious, amazing moment.

And now Joe's mother held Jacko's hand as the minister stepped forward.

Joe caught Ellie's eye and they both smiled. They'd taken a very roundabout way to reach this point, but the rough and rugged journey had been worth it. They knew there'd be more bends in the road ahead, but that was OK as they'd be travelling together. Always.

* * * * *

Mills & Boon® Hardback

December 2013

ROMANCE

Defiant in the Desert	Sharon Kendrick
Not Just the Boss's Plaything	Caitlin Crews
Rumours on the Red Carpet	Carole Mortimer
The Change in Di Navarra's Plan	Lynn Raye Harris
The Prince She Never Knew	Kate Hewitt
His Ultimate Prize	Maya Blake
More than a Convenient Marriage?	Dani Collins
A Hunger for the Forbidden	Maisey Yates
The Reunion Lie	Lucy King
The Most Expensive Night of Her Life	Amy Andrews
Second Chance with Her Soldier	Barbara Hannay
Snowed in with the Billionaire	Caroline Anderson
Christmas at the Castle	Marion Lennox
Snowflakes and Silver Linings	Cara Colter
Beware of the Boss	Leah Ashton
Too Much of a Good Thing?	Joss Wood
After the Christmas Party...	Janice Lynn
Date with a Surgeon Prince	Meredith Webber

MEDICAL

From Venice with Love	Alison Roberts
Christmas with Her Ex	Fiona McArthur
Her Mistletoe Wish	Lucy Clark
Once Upon a Christmas Night...	Annie Claydon

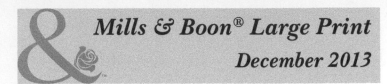

Mills & Boon® Large Print

December 2013

ROMANCE

The Billionaire's Trophy	Lynne Graham
Prince of Secrets	Lucy Monroe
A Royal Without Rules	Caitlin Crews
A Deal with Di Capua	Cathy Williams
Imprisoned by a Vow	Annie West
Duty at What Cost?	Michelle Conder
The Rings That Bind	Michelle Smart
A Marriage Made in Italy	Rebecca Winters
Miracle in Bellaroo Creek	Barbara Hannay
The Courage To Say Yes	Barbara Wallace
Last-Minute Bridesmaid	Nina Harrington

HISTORICAL

Not Just a Governess	Carole Mortimer
A Lady Dares	Bronwyn Scott
Bought for Revenge	Sarah Mallory
To Sin with a Viking	Michelle Willingham
The Black Sheep's Return	Elizabeth Beacon

MEDICAL

NYC Angels: Making the Surgeon Smile	Lynne Marshall
NYC Angels: An Explosive Reunion	Alison Roberts
The Secret in His Heart	Caroline Anderson
The ER's Newest Dad	Janice Lynn
One Night She Would Never Forget	Amy Andrews
When the Cameras Stop Rolling...	Connie Cox

Mills & Boon® Hardback

January 2014

ROMANCE

MEDICAL

Mills & Boon® Large Print
January 2014

ROMANCE

Challenging Dante	Lynne Graham
Captivated by Her Innocence	Kim Lawrence
Lost to the Desert Warrior	Sarah Morgan
His Unexpected Legacy	Chantelle Shaw
Never Say No to a Caffarelli	Melanie Milburne
His Ring Is Not Enough	Maisey Yates
A Reputation to Uphold	Victoria Parker
Bound by a Baby	Kate Hardy
In the Line of Duty	Ami Weaver
Patchwork Family in the Outback	Soraya Lane
The Rebound Guy	Fiona Harper

HISTORICAL

Mistress at Midnight	Sophia James
The Runaway Countess	Amanda McCabe
In the Commodore's Hands	Mary Nichols
Promised to the Crusader	Anne Herries
Beauty and the Baron	Deborah Hale

MEDICAL

Dr Dark and Far-Too Delicious	Carol Marinelli
Secrets of a Career Girl	Carol Marinelli
The Gift of a Child	Sue MacKay
How to Resist a Heartbreaker	Louisa George
A Date with the Ice Princess	Kate Hardy
The Rebel Who Loved Her	Jennifer Taylor

Mills & Boon® Online

Discover more romance at
www.millsandboon.co.uk

- **FREE** online reads
- **Books** up to one month before shops
- **Browse our books** before you buy

...and much more!

For exclusive competitions and instant updates:

 Like us on **facebook.com/millsandboon**

 Follow us on **twitter.com/millsandboon**

 Join us on **community.millsandboon.co.uk**

Visit us Online Sign up for our FREE eNewsletter at **www.millsandboon.co.uk**

WEB/M&B/RTL5/HB